Scrooge in Love

A Novel

by

John Killinger

ISBN Paperback: 978-1-963701-89-0
ISBN Hardcover: 978-1-963701-92-0
ISBN E-Book: 978-1-963701-93-7

First Edition

Published by Freiling Agency
Warrenton, VA
www.freilingagency.com

Contents

Chapter 1

A Glowing Spirit

It would be hard indeed, even if one were to live to a ripe old age, to know another person whose spirit of life and generosity underwent a change as dramatic as that of Ebenezer Scrooge. Many who had known him for years failed to recognize him in the street or shops, his conversion had been so sudden and revolutionary. He often wh13ooped and sang as he walked along, so pleased was he with the alteration of his inner feelings. People who had known him man and boy could hardly believe it was he, so completely transformed was he in both manner and appearance.

To begin with, there was a never-flagging glow of human warmth about him that seemed to compel him to speak kindly and affectionately to all he met, whether he had been acquainted with them or not. He appeared genuinely concerned for the welfare of all, to the effect that he not only wore a mien of sincere and loving solicitousness, but bore in his pockets an impressive wad of bank notes from which he readily removed a few to place in the hands of those whose most pressing need was for a little help in paying their rent or putting food upon the table. It was a wonder he did not soon bankrupt himself and the business of

1

Scrooge and Marley, of which he was the sole surviving partner, and yet there seemed to be an endless supply of bills, as if it expanded daily through the very act of sharing.

And his behavior toward those with whom he was most closely associated, why, that was the most extraordinary of all! One could even say, without any fear of exaggeration, that he produced a glow of happiness amongst them that was like the very sunlight itself! Within a fortnight of that fateful Christmas eve on which he received the extraordinary visits of three immortal spirits, he had brought his nephew Fred McDougall, his dear, departed sister's son, into business with him as the new president of the company, and had promoted Robert Cratchit, the sweet-spirited "Bob," his long-suffering accountant, into the position of vice president, a rise so precipitous, and involving such a raise in pay, that his dear wife, the voluble Mrs. Cratchit, pinched herself a thousand times a day in joyous awe and disbelief.

"Together," Scrooge declared to them, "we shall make of this enterprise so great a success that it will bless not only us but half the people of this empire, for we shall be always mindful, or I will at least, who have most of which to testify, of the generous God who spares us day by day and graciously endows us with the means whereby we can make other people happy. That shall be our motto, boys, to make other people happy, and we shall spare nothing, leave no stone unturned and no effort unattended, to realize this blessed aim. When we come to work each day, it will not be as sullen galley slaves returning to their heavy oars, but as the angels in heaven themselves entering the storehouse of the

Almighty, wherein it is their glorious duty to pour out pails of gold and silver for the poor mortals who dwell upon the earth! So shall it be, or I shall have failed in my pledge and loyalty to the very Spirit of Christmas to whom I owe not only my life but the delirious song in my heart and unaccustomed spring in my step! I charge you, boys, for the sake of old Ebenezer himself and the lives of all of those upon whose his is privileged to impinge, let us, in every way possible, keep Christmas alive throughout the year, and extend its wondrous air and bounty to every soul we meet!"

Thus it was, and the air within the firm of Marley, Scrooge, McDougall, & Cratchit, as it was now called, seemed to hum with a radiance and vitality that drew new customers in by the droves. Soon, upon the urging of his imaginative nephew and the industrious Bob Cratchit, the firm had expanded in a dozen ways, offering brokerage service, insurance, new product development, building construction, mine safety products, mineral exploration, and general management, along with an interest in several kinds of charities for the betterment of the poor, the sick, the orphaned, and the handicapped. Those who had once called old Scrooge by the vilest of names now spoke of him as if he were a saint, and his name was often uttered in Sunday sermons as if synonymous with that of the good Lord himself. For several years a major newspaper ran a tally of the vast number of children born in local hospitals and birthing institutions who had, in his honor, had bestowed upon them the name of Ebenezer. Some enterprising parents had even christened their infant daughters with such derivative appellations as Bena or Ebena, which were roundly believed to be conducive in those children to a generous and loving spirit.

Scrooge, who had had no family at all to speak of, or at least none to which he paid acknowledgement, now had many families.

First, there were his nephew and his nephew's wife, who welcomed him into their home as often as he could be persuaded to dine with them, and always served him with their finest china and freshly polished silverware, convinced that in his new incarnation he was somehow close to deity.

Then, there were the Cratchits, Bob's dear and lively brood, who invariably celebrated his advent with cheerfulness and laughter, so that there was an atmosphere of heavenly bliss whenever he crossed the threshold. Four of the Cratchit brood were now employed in the offices of Marley, Scrooge, McDougall, & Cratchit, in addition to Bob himself – the eldest son, Peter, the eldest daughter, Martha, who had experience in accounting, young Tiny Tim, who, now that he was in better health from the finest medical help, was useful in running errands, and Mrs. Cratchit herself, who had quit her previous cleaning job to turn her significant attention to the firm's expanding offices, though in light of Bob's munificent salary she refused to take a penny for her labors, so that Scrooge had to reward her in other, more subtle, ways, with little gifts of food or flowers or sometimes a beautiful frock or bottle of French perfume. There were also all the other families now attached to the firm by virtue of one or another of some family member's involvement in the business.

And last, but far from least, there was the family of Scrooge's fellow church members, for he had now become a regular attender and generous benefactor of his nearest neighborhood religious establishment, St. Martin's in the Swale, with the result that the rector had pressed upon him the duty of becoming a deacon and serving on the church board, in which position he was admirably suited to guide the congregation into a kind of prosperity it had never before enjoyed. Scrooge liked the Rev. Mr. Josiah Plumwood, who had a manner as kind and considerate as any woman's, and his wife, Mrs. Plumwood, who was as short and plump as her husband was tall and slender. Together, they were a welcoming committee as warm and friendly as a brass band on a cold day, and they set a tone that seemed to pervade the entire congregation, for everybody who worshipped at St. Martin's appeared to be generous and accepting. Scrooge even attended the Wednesday night dinners in the church hall, where many proud housewives brought their favorite dishes to be savored especially by him, and by Rev. Plumwood too, of course, and would have been sorely disappointed had the two of them not felt well enough to indulge themselves in at least a small portion of these carefully prepared and elaborately displayed delicacies. Each man confessed to the other, after a few months of this royal treatment, that he had resolved not to eat a bite of solid food on Thursdays after, in order that the ritual of the Wednesday evening meal should not lead to the inevitable putting on of weight it would have otherwise entailed.

In this aura of manifold blessedness, Scrooge recalled the one day of the year when he had once experienced anything like it, those Christmas eves when he worked for old Mr. Fezziwig and his employer

staged the great parties and dances to which they all looked forward the first eleven and a half monthsof every year. Marley, Scrooge, McDougall, & Cratchit, he declared, should have a similar annual party. No, a single annual party was not enough, he thought, to express the liberality of spirit to which he had soon become addicted. So he announced, instead, that Marley, Scrooge, McDougall, & Cratchit should have not one but two such parties each and every year, and decreed that the second party, or first, depending on which way one calculated the dates, should take place on May the First, a venerable English holiday stemming from the ancient revelries associated with the arrival of Spring.

As there was no hall within Marley, Scrooge, McDougall, and Cratchit's current quarters sufficient to hold for such a party the large staff of people now employed by the firm, plus of course their families and special friends, Scrooge determined that they should acquire more suitable accommodations. A huge warehouse barely six blocks away from their present address, one that had lain idle now for several seasons owing to the demise of its former owner and a court dispute that had held up its final disposition, provided the very answer Scrooge had sought, and, with a total makeover accomplished by the firm's own construction crew, aided by the esthetic eye of young Martha Cratchit, it became a great shining jewel within the architectural setting of its general environment, occasioning a general sprucing up of the entire area, the other proprietors feeling heartily ashamed of having let their properties decay into such a moribund condition. The new hall within this prosperous establishment became a much- coveted setting for grand events, so that the firm occasionally lent it out for rival companies to have their parties and inaugurations. But it was always reserved, on the May the First and the twenty-fourth of December, for the eager staff and families of Marley, Scrooge, McDougall, & Cratchit, who filled it near-to-bursting with boisterous fun, delicious food, plentiful drink, and a spirit of gaiety whose like would be hard to find. There was always a bit of ceremony to inaugurate a party or performance, and also music in abundance, often provided by Tiny Tim and a band of his young friends who played on horns and drums and fifes and harps. Then Fred McDougall and his beautiful wife Nessa would commence the dance, followed by Bob Cratchit and Mrs. Cratchit, and eventually, somewhere in the queue of revelers, old Scrooge himself, accompanied by whichever fair young maiden was lucky enough to invite him first to join her in the jigs and reels, which would go on until nearly daybreak for those hardy enough to continue at such an active pace. Food was continuously supplied by a staff of obliging caterers, and good ale flowed like heavenly nectar from dozens of clever, ever-bubbling fountains arranged about the room. As the next day was always a Sabbath or a holiday, and sometimes both, there was no need to discontinue the revelry until the hardiest of participants had ceased to dance, and confessed themselves exhausted in the joyous and riotous expenditure of energy.

Scrooge always pondered, on these magnificent occasions, the great happiness he had felt as a young employee in Mr. Fezziwig's company, when he and Miss Annabelle Fezziwig had danced the reels together, each tireless and unwearied in the bloom of mutual love and adoration, and had sometimes sat

together on the side as others danced, holding hands and dreaming of a time when they would marry and have a family of their own. But with the remembering came also a sense of shame, that he had allowed his ambition for wealth and status to overtake and then eclipse his joy in Annabelle herself. It was innocent enough, in the beginning, for he persuaded himself it was for her sake he wanted these things, so that she would be proud of him and feel as secure in his household as she had in the home of her industrious father. But his avarice had grown completely out of hand, so that eventually she had seen it and called it what it was, an idolatry of gold, and had told him that she could no longer compete with such a mistress and was therefore returning the ring he had given her to seal the fact of their engagement. That had been a shock to young Ebenezer Scrooge's pride, more than to his heart, for she was right, he had become addicted to work and the sense of power it bought him. It wasn't long before his disappointment at losing Miss Fezziwig had been absorbed in the pleasure of his achievements, for he and Jacob Marley, another aspiring young businessman he had met in the exchange, contrived by their joint efforts to found a new lending company, Scrooge and Marley, that was soon one of the most prosperous firms of its kind in the city of London. If he thought at all of what he had lost, it was always for only a fleeting moment, instantly dismissed by the return of his mind to the magnetic center of all his being, the creation of wealth. Now, however, in his transformed state, he found that thoughts of Annabelle came upon him with increasing frequency, and he often wondered what had become of her, and whether she had been happy and fulfilled by her marriage to another, a chap whose name he perhaps once heard but just as quickly dismissed, for by then, he believed, it was already water under the bridge. Had they had children, he questioned, and were those children grown by now? She had surely inherited a reasonable fortune when her father passed on, as, given his age, he must have done a number of years ago. She had two brothers, Scrooge knew, for he had worked beside them in the business. One was keen, he recalled, but the other was something of an idiot and a wastrel. Surely old Fezziwig had passed the business onto the children when he retired, and he and Mrs. Fezziwig had lived in quiet contentment in their declining years. Scrooge realized that, in spite of all the happiness he was now finding in his altered state of existence, he too was in the declining years, the twilight time of life when darkness was bound to fall in the not-too-distant future. It would be nice, at such a time, to have a loving wife by his side, someone with whom to reminisce about the past, to remark upon present happenings and stand guard against the multiple hazards of old age. More and more, he found himself daydreaming of Annabelle, and wondering if she was even still alive. She must be white-haired by now, as he was, and a little less certain in her gait, as he also was. She might huff and puff after the exertion of climbing the stairs or walking a few blocks to bring home a basket of groceries. Would she have kept her girlish figure, or, as in his own case, would she have put on some careless pounds, so that she was now what people affectionately referred to as "pleasantly plump"?

Sometimes he dreamed about her at night as well, and would awaken with the sharp pang of desire in his heart, a longing to see her and touch her hand and talk to her of all the years they had missed together, in spite of whatever happiness each now found in their present status. He put great store in dreams, after those blessed revelations effected in his life by the visits of the Christmas spirits, for he was never quite sure whether the spirits had come in actuality or via the medium of dreams. Either way, he knew, it made no difference, for whichever way it was had thoroughly affected the course of his existence. To dream of Annabelle began to seem more and more fortuitous to him, as if some inner consciousness were dawning and could not be put off, as if heaven itself were trying to tell him something about the woman he had once held so dear, before his thoughts were diverted to other, less meaningful idols of the heart. Accordingly, one day, a few hours after having enjoyed a particularly vivid dream of Annabelle, one he could not shake after his morning coffee and attention to a number of items of business waiting for him on his desk, he wandered into the office of a private detective whose sign he had beheld a few blocks away from the headquarters of Marley, Scrooge, McDougall, & Cratchit. It took him but a few moments to find the place, for he had marked it more certainly while passing it of late, and perhaps in his inner mind registered its existence for such a time as this. "R. Dooley," said the sign as he now fixed his eye upon it, "Private Investigations Undertaken with Absolute Discretion."

Mr. Dooley turned out to be a middle-aged Irishman, portly, bald, and somewhat down at the heels in his appearance, for his cuffs were frayed and his shoe soles obviously stood in need of vital repair. The thin brown hair on the right side of his head he allowed to grow quite long, and then brushed it over his baldness to the other side, pomading it with a greasy substance capable of holding it in place on any but the windiest of days. His cheeks were round and chubby, and his neck rose in heavy folds from his shirt, collapsing, at the bottom tier, over the sides of his collar. But his handshake was firm and inspiring of confidence, as was his way of looking a client in the eye when he spoke, for his orbs were dark and penetrating, excellent eyes, Scrooge thought, for looking into other people's affairs and ferreting out secrets. "I have a mission for you," said Scrooge without delay, once they had made their introductions, "and it is very important to me. I shall gladly pay your fee and your expenses for an assignment that should take an experienced man like yourself but a few days to sort out." And he described for Dooley the little that he knew about Annabelle – her name before she was married, her father's business and his sons' names, and how she looked at the time when he knew her, although he realized she must now be greatly changed if still alive at all.

"I'd like you to be very discreet," said Scrooge, "in fact, the artful soul of discretion. If you can find her yet existing, do not divulge to her the name of your employer, but discover, if you can, her present status and address. That is all I require, nothing more. No gossip. No scandal. Merely her health, her family situation – by that, I mean whether she is married and has children – and where she lives."

"I understand," said Mr. Dooley, a knowing twinkle in his eye and a finger laid alongside his nose. "She, Mrs. Annabelle Fezziwig X, will not even know that Robert Dooley exists, I shall be so discreet. And I shall seek you out immediately, Mr.

Scrooge, as soon as I have anything to report." One of Scrooge's many undertakings, in the months following his glorious transformation, was to commission the design and erection of an elegant, large, and expensive mausoleum for his former partner, Jacob Marley. It was to Marley, he felt, that he owed the extreme joy and happiness of his present condition; for if Marley had not come to him on that fateful Christmas eve and admonished him about the approach of the three spirits that whisked Scrooge away on those unbelievable journeys of the soul, he did not believe he would have even met the spirits; and without them, he would have soon died of dyspepsia, stress, or self-inflicted biliousness, and would not have entered upon the remarkable period of general euphoria that had marked his existence ever since.

He still retained, on the front door of his dwelling place, that figure of a knocker that once had somehow metamorphosed into the face of his old partner, for he treasured it above all evaluation, not for its intrinsic worth, of course, but for its associations with that Christmas eve when his fabulous transformation had taken place. But Marley, he felt, should have a much more respectable monument than was afforded by his momentary visage on a door knocker, so Scrooge purchased several burial plots within the fashionable cemetery where he wished the mausoleum to be erected, ordered the monument to be situated in the middle of them, and requested a heavy iron chain to be strung along a number of standards around the perimeter of the plots, with neatly groomed sod covering all of it except the monument itself. He commissioned one of the best statuary artists of the city to create a likeness of Jacob Marley from two or three sepia-toned photographs remaining, plus Scrooge's own recollection of him which was refreshed by that nocturnal visit, and commanded that the statue, standing considerably taller than life – between eight and ten feet in height, he thought would be best – be placed on a short pedestal at the front opening of the mausoleum. The result was quite striking, he believed, as if old Jacob were standing at his own front door, about to greet any friends passing by and usher them across the threshold of his home. Everyone said the effect was very fortuitous, and the businessmen who had known and visited with Marley on the floor of the stock exchange declared it to be one of the finest monuments in the country. The statuary artist, in fact, said jokingly, "Mr. Scrooge, sir, I should give you a discount on my work because it has resulted in my receiving so many new commissions."

"On the contrary," said the highly pleased Scrooge, "you should increase the price, for it means that you have done an exceptionally fine job on the commission you had from me!

From the first, Scrooge liked to stroll over to the cemetery in the evenings, when the neighborhood was quiet and the street gaslights burned softly in the gloaming, to sit on a stone bench he had commanded to be fashioned and set within the chain fence and commune with the spirit of his old friend Marley. Nothing in the way of decipherable speech passed between them, of course, but Scrooge fancied that the two of them were joined in quiet discourse, for he himself often recounted to Marley's statue the events of his day – whom he had encountered, what they had said, and how it had been another in an endless array of wonderful days touched off by Marley's visit on that fateful Christmas eve, for which he never ceased to thank his erstwhile partner. Now he even confessed to Marley that he had hired an investigator to look into the present whereabouts and fortunes of his old friend Annabelle Fezziwig, whom Marley had known slightly because he had been a friend of the man who eventually married the girl. "I know it sounds crazy," Scrooge said, "but I can't stop thinking about her, Jacob. I know now what a mistake it was when I let her go because I was more interested in making my fortune than in establishing a family with her."

Marley, he imagined, tacitly agreed with him, even though the statue said not a word. As each year drew on and the weather became more inclement and very much colder, he ceased to go as often, but he made a point of revisiting the monument every Christmas Eve, something he considered almost a sacred pilgrimage, for it always reminded him with particular force of his visit with Marley on the Christmas eve that changed his life. Leaving Marley, Scrooge, McDougall, & Cratchit's lively Christmas party, he would bundle up in his great coat, with a warm scarf around his neck and earmuffs beneath his top hat, and take up his position on the cemetery bench like a sentry watching over some important site. There he would sit until he had carefully rehearsed the events of that storied Christmas eve – the appearances of the three ghosts, his visits to his childhood home and school, Fezziwig's party, the Cratchit household, his nephew's dinner, his break-up with Annabelle, the cemetery where he found his own name upon a tombstone – and then, tears running down his craggy old face, he would express his profuse thanks once more to his dear friend and partner for the role he had performed in Scrooge's salvation from a sad half-life of bitterness and desiccation. Then he would sit a few minutes more, sometimes with minute icicles forming at the tip of his nose, as if waiting for any further communication from his former partner, and finally he would stand, pause a moment longer, then turn and walk quietly back to his abode, where he would say his prayers and clamber into bed for a few hours' rest before commencing his many visitations on Christmas day. One Monday morning, on an exceedingly dreary and blustery day in early November, Scrooge's nephew, Fred McDougall, tapped at his office door and asked if he might come in. "Of course!" said Scrooge, always happy for an opportunity to see his kinsman, who was now almost always extremely busy with his weighty assignment as head of a thriving multi-national business operation. "My door is always open to you, Fred. You know that."

"What's on your mind?" he asked as Fred sat tentatively near the front of the easy chair beside Scrooge's desk. "Are you not feeling well, my boy?" Fred shrugged off the question.

"There's something going on in the firm, Uncle," he said. "I haven't got all the facts yet, but I'm working on it. I'm afraid somebody is stealing from us."

Scrooge regarded him soberly, but not unpleasantly, as he would have done at similar news a few years back. "You seem to think it's very serious," he said, " or you would not look so ill."

"It is, Uncle. I'm afraid it is."

Chapter 2

The Cratchit Family

"Well, my boy," said Scrooge, "you'll sort it out. I know you will. I have every confidence in you. And Fred?"

" Yes, Uncle."

"Come back to me when you know what it is. Maybe it's somebody who got in a momentary bind of a sort. You know how it is – an overdue draft, an illness in the family, a little spot of trouble. There are dozens of reasons somebody"might fiddle the books or take a few bob from the cash register. It happens under the best of circumstances. Try not to let it upset you too much, whatever it is."

Fred smiled a half-hearted smile. Sometimes he had to pinch himself to believe this man was his real Uncle Scrooge, for he was not at all like the Uncle Scrooge he could still remember if he tried very hard, the one reported to have said of the poor who were ill and in need of medical help, "Let them die and decrease the surplus population." Look at him there, thought Fred. He's the very picture of serenity and acceptance, not a bit like the tough-as-nails, storm-the-battlements-and-give-them-no-mercy uncle he once encountered in the offices of Scrooge and Marley.

"Fred," said Scrooge.

"Yes, Uncle?"

"It has been too long, you know."

"Too long – for what?" He wondered if he had offended his relative by being tardy with some report or failing to deal with an errant matter he could not even bring to mind.

"Too long since you and Nessa and I had dinner at some new restaurant. I'm afraid we've been letting this business get in the way of our celebrating life the way we were meant to do. I've heard of a new little French place that's all the rage. What's it called, Chez Dauphin? Do you know it? Haven't been there, have you?"

"No, Uncle." "Then let's waste no more time in visiting it! What do you say? Would a week from Friday evening be good for you and Nessa?"

Fred smiled, genuinely, for the first time since entering Scrooge's office. "Of course, Uncle," he said. "Let's do it! I'll tell Nessa tonight. She'll be thrilled. She has a new dress she's been dying to wear, and this will be the perfect opportunity."

"Wonderful," said his uncle. "What color is her dress, by the way?"

"Purple, I think."

"Great," said Scrooge. "She'll be beautiful in that color. In any color, for that matter, but especially in purple." And he made a mental note to order a white corsage from the little woman with a flower shop around the corner, with a ribbon to complement a purple dress.

Eleven days from the day that Scrooge had first entered his office, Robert Dooley came to call upon him in his own office at Marley, Scrooge, McDougall, & Cratchit.

"Ah, Mr. Dooley," said Scrooge with obvious pleasure at seeing him again. "Come in, come in! Have a cigar, won't you?" he asked, proferring a jar of Havanas whose aroma, when Scrooge lifted the top, could not be described as anything less than "heavenly."

Mr. Dooley took a cigar, had a seat, and with deliberate calm bit the end off the cigar, spat it into his hand, and transferred it to his own coat pocket. A tiny smirk played at the corners of his mouth, as if to announce beforehand that he believed he had been successful in his mission.

"I can see you are pleased," said Scrooge. "You have the air of a cat who has caught a nice fat mouse by the tail."

Dooley's head bobbed slowly up and down as he lit the cigar and proceeded to puff on it, letting the aromatic smoke drift lazily from his nostrils. He removed the cigar, looked at it approvingly, then replaced it in his mouth.

"You might well say that, Mr. Scrooge," he said at last. "Yes, indeed, you might well say it, for I think I have just the information you have been seeking."

"Wonderful," said Scrooge, his face alight with pleasure. "I am all ears, Mr. Dooley."

"Well," said Dooley, removing a small black notebook from his pocket and, turning its pages with the hand in which he held the cigar between his fingers, as deftly as if he did this very act a dozen times a day, stopped at last, and, with his finger on a particular page, took a pair of small wire-rimmed spectacles from his vest pocket, the better to read what he had written there. By this time, he had made the word "well" sound as if it were several syllables in length, but now he was ready to take another puff from the cigar, let the smoke wend its way from his nostrils, and proceed to impart the information he had garnered.

"Mistress Annabelle Fezziwig Moore," he said, very slowly and deliberately, announcing each name with all due gravity, but especially the last one, which he then repeated in an even more thoughtful tone. "Now residing at 128 1/2 Outer" Lane in Kensington. Husband, Arthur Gerald Moore, a printer, deceased. Two children, both daughters, survive the father. Celia, 28, married to Delbert Newsome Crane, living in Oxford. Margaret, 26, married to Sgt. Jonathan Hennessy, now deceased. Missus Hennessy lives in the village of Shelburne, where she is employed as a milliner's assistant.

"Ah, Mr. Dooley," said Scrooge with an air of great satisfaction, "you have done well, as I expected you would. I am very pleased to have the information you have just given me."

"Have another cigar," he said, proffering the jar, "and if you will provide me with your bill, I shall see that you are paid before you leave the building."

Mr. Dooley, reaching for another smoke, said "Thankee, sir," his broad, fat face redistributed into a glowing smile of self-approbation. "Any time, sir. Any time at all!"

Chapter 3

Marley's Monument

Finally Rings the Belle Young Ebenezer Scrooge had been blissfully in love with young Annabelle Fezziwig, whom he usually called simply Belle, as she was known to her family and close friends. He had experienced the sense of fullness and ecstasy that most young swains feel when they first fall in love, thinking of little else but how to please and enjoy the company of the object of his desire. She had loved him with a similar passion in return. To watch them in the hallway at old Fezziwig's offices was entertainment itself. They often managed to brush against one another furtively in passing and at other times merely stood gazing into one another's eyes, as if staring into the mysteries at the center of life itself. When they knew they were alone, as they sometimes were in the stock room if both happened to go for supplies at the same time, they dared to touch their hands briefly, and occasionally even to brush their lips together in a gentle and tender motion. Once, on a picnic in the countryside with the entire Fezziwig family, they took off their shoes and stockings and dangled their bare feet in the small creek running through the pasture, and touched their wet toes and ankles in promiscuous disregard of her parents, scarcely a hundred yards away beneath the gracious shade of a wide-spreading oak. Neither was really responsible for asking the other to marry. Their agreement was simply the product of an inner acquiescence, a mutual feeling that metamorphosed into an understanding that they expected to be realized as soon as Ebenezer had set by enough money to make it feasible to establish a household of their own. Each was happy with that casual, unspoken arrangement, and lived in joyful anticipation of the time when it would be fulfilled. Annabelle's parents were well satisfied with her choice – they could not help but know, even though she never once spoke openly to them of the relationship – and conspired with the young people in dreaming of a day when Ebenezer, whose own parents were dead, would become an intimate part of their family. Fezziwig even thought of the perfect wedding gift: on the day of their nuptials, he would make young Ebenezer a full partner in his business! Then Ebenezer, caught up in the greed that overtakes us when we least expect it, began to think more and more of making money and less and less of enjoying the company of Annabelle. She noticed it, of course, but at first assumed it was only a passing phase, soon to be discarded for his old persona, that of a simple, adoring suitor. When this did not happen, she anguished over what to do. Her usual innocent coquetry no longer proved sufficient to stem the tide of his fascination with business. So finally, in desperation, she made her decision and told him that she no longer wished to marry him because he had changed and was not the young man she once knew. Ebenezer was only briefly chagrined by this announcement, for he had become so seduced by the world of the marketplace that he barely noticed the change in his life, and soon he was working again full throttle, even in the evenings, which he would formerly have spent with

Annabelle.

Now, all these years later, he felt awkward and embarrassed to be ferreting her out and showing up on her doorstep at 128 1/2 Outer Lane, bearing a bouquet of colorful freesias, which he remembered had once been her very favorite flowers. The house was a modest one, but in a comfortable old neighborhood. Like most of the houses on Outer Lane, it boasted no expansive porch, but only a doorstep under a small overhanging roof. He wished for a greater cover, something to hide him from what he imagined were the peering eyes and curious speculations of neighbors or passersby. But he had buttressed his courage during the cab ride across the city, and now he reached for the doorbell with a determination born of a thousand dreams of beholding his old sweetheart at least one more time.

Intent on seeing Annabelle as an elderly woman, or at least one as mature as he himself now was, he was surprised when the door was answered by a girl of eighteen or nineteen who looked him boldly in the face and, without uttering a single word, managed to mime upon her countenance the question of his purpose for standing there, for she had never laid eyes on him before.

"Uh – ah –," he stuttered, not having anticipated the situation, "your mistress? Is this the home of Missus Annabelle Moore?"

By now the girl was staring at the large bundle of freesias, and the curiosity on her face congealed into a more-or-less permanent stare.

"It is," she said, and waited for him to amplify his purpose.

"Is she at home?" said Scrooge. "I would like to see her, if you please." Without speaking, the girl stepped back, opening the door a bit wider as she did so, and nodded for him to move into the entryway. Then she shut the door and left him among a coat tree, a mirror stand, and an umbrella box with the staffs of several umbrellas poking out as she herself opened and entered a doorway to the right. A glimpse into the room as she went through revealed to him a blazing fire in a small but attractive fireplace surrounded by glazed tiles, with a mirror in a gold-colored frame above it and a bouquet of dried flowers upon the mantel, and he imagined that Annabelle was seated on a sofa opposite, perhaps with needlework across her lap, or else a book that she was in the midst of reading. "There's a gentleman asking to see you, ma'am," he heard the young woman say, and then the voice of a mature woman, strong and firm, yet attractively lilting and musical, replied, "You may show him in, Ginnie."

At that instant, something inside Scrooge wished to bolt, to whirl and exit before the young woman had had a chance to return to the hallway and bid him enter, but that urging was quickly stifled by another, stronger impulse eager to behold the face that went with the voice, the countenance of one he had loved as a youngster but that would now present itself as nature had rendered it after a journey of

years. He thought his heart would beat quite through his vest as he followed the girl into the room and first laid eyes upon the face and form of her he had so desperately longed to see again. Then he was feeling the warmth from the fire, bowing slightly from the waist, and handing the flowers to Annabelle as he asked, in a low, supplicative voice, "Do you remember me, Belle? It's Ebenezer. Ebenezer Scrooge."

For a moment, silence hung in the room as a quizzical look passed across her visage. Scrooge held his breath in fear of some amnesia on her part that might have dismissed him years ago.

"Ebenezer?" she said. "Ebenezer Scrooge? Is it really you? Can it be, after all these years?" He knew, the moment he heard that mellifluous voice, so full and free and generous, so comforting and embracing in its tones, that he loved her still, and more than ever, if that be possible. "It is, my dear. It is," he said as his eyes locked upon hers and he knelt on one knee before her, taking her free hand in both of his and pressing it against his cheek.

Later, he would piece together his heart's reactions at beholding her again, and how remarkably beautiful she remained after the passage of so many years. Her figure had become a little more ample, but somehow, he thought, it suited her. Her face was a portrait of loveliness and kindness, and he saw in it traces of both her parents, whom he so fondly remembered. What happened in the next few seconds, how he rose to his feet, removed his great coat and handed it, with his hat and scarf, to the girl Ginnie, who had followed him in, he would never know. But he would never forget, by the same token, what followed that, as Annabelle rose to her feet and the two of them became lost in a grand embrace, so that he smelled the subtle perfume she had dabbed beneath her ear, together with the gentle aroma of the soap she had used upon her hands and face. It was one of those supremely timeless and fulfilling moments, when the passing years were banished and the two of them stood soul to soul, like heavenly creatures gifted with the power to meld together into one and then withdraw, savoring that they had touched.

"Oh, Ebbie," she cooed, echoing the name she had called him all those years before, "I am so glad to see you! You'll never believe it. Ten minutes ago, as I sat here sorting through these old photographs, I thought of you and developed an incredible yearning to see you. There was a picture of you that you had had made especially for me, or so you said. You were wearing one of those old fashioned stiff collars, remember? And a tie and coat. And you were standing there very sober and formal, as if you were at a funeral. I laughed when I saw the pose, but I did so long to see you. Can you believe it? And here you are, like a genie out of the bottle! I feel as if I have been granted a special wish, as if God himself had reached down into this very room and given me a blessing far beyond my worth or expectation. I must pinch myself to see if you are really here!"

At once they were laughing and talking so eagerly that first one stopped and then the other, and then both began again, chirping like two school girls who had not seen one another over the school holidays but were now reunited and in full spate of conversation. There was so much to say, so much to tell about what had transpired, that before they knew it the sun had set and darkness fallen, and yet they continued as eager as ever, sharing now this, now that token ofinformation, until the hiss of ashes falling into the glowing embers bade them remember the time and the necessity of more coal upon the grate.

"You'll stay for tea?" she said. "But it's way past tea time. Perhaps a bit of supper. Please, dear Ebbie, say you will!"

"If it's no trouble," he replied, eager to remain.

"Oh no, it's no trouble at all," she said, picking up the little brass bell from an end table and ringing it gently.

"Ginnie. Mr. Scrooge will take supper with me this evening. Can you provide some sandwiches, perhaps, and a bit of soup or something hot? And a pot of tea, of course, and some biscuits. Can you do that, dear?"

"Of course, ma'am," said the girl, stooping to hoist the coal bucket and drop some coals upon the grate. "In the dining room or here by the fire?"

"Here, I think," said her mistress.

So the talk continued. They remembered details about her parents' life and old Fezziwig's parties. She told Scrooge about her husband – how they had met, what a kind but ineffectual man he was, for which she valued him all the more, and how sick he had been at the last, when she had often been up all night tending to his needs and once falling ill herself from over-expended effort. She glowed as she described her daughters, Celia and Margaret, and their accomplishments, and he saw her countenance darken as she thought of Margaret and how she had lost her husband Jonathan so young, a tragedy enhanced by the fact that they had been so deeply and enthusiastically in love. She pried from Scrooge the details of his life in the years after they parted—how exclusively he had applied himself to business, so that he became one of the largest property owners in the city and therefore spent a lot of time collecting rents and deposits from his tenants. Caught up in the spirit of their sharing, he admitted that it had been mainly an empty and sterile period in his existence, when he might as well have lived in some black and airless hole without connection to the outside world. He omitted telling her about his conversion that fateful Christmas eve, as it would have taken too long to explain everything, but looked forward to sharing it at a later time.

They talked about their health, now that they were both on in years, and how their bodies were beginning to protest the strain of all that living. She had some palpitations of the heart and a knee that sometimes gave way when she least expected it to do so. He confessed to having had some trouble with his own heart, but said that it had been much better in recent years. Both admitted that their joints started feeling stiff and painful whenever a weather front approached, and they mentioned a little problem with their memories, which had a terrible habit of deserting them at just the moments when they needed them most. Still, they agreed they were in quite passable condition, considering the decades they had seen.

"Did you never think to marry?" Annabelle inquired.

Scrooge looked into the fire, where the coals were now burning with new zest. "No," he answered truthfully. "There was never anyone but you, Belle." But surely there were women who were attracted to what you could give them?"

He smiled wryly and shook his head no. "If there were, I didn't pay any attention to them," he said. "I had failed with the best, and wouldn't risk it with a lesser woman than yourself."

At one point, Ginnie looked in to see if she should bid her mistress goodnight before ascending the stairs to her little room, but they were so engrossed in conversation, so animated and effervescent, that she hesitated and quietly climbed the stairs without distracting them.

They were still talking when the coals had burned down again and some ancient neighborhood clock struck ten. "I'm sorry, Belle," he murmured, "I have stayed beyond your bedtime, I'm sure."

Chapter 4

Searching for Annabelle

She dismissed his apology with a toss of her head, smiling, and said, "I'll let you go for now, Ebbie, but you must promise to come again, and soon."

Scrooge had to walk several blocks to a cab stand, but was glad to do it, for the pleasure exploding in his veins needed the exercise of such a distance. Had anyone seen him under a streetlamp as he passed, they would have thought him inebriated, for he weaved this way and that, singing a little tune, and once, in an exuberance of sheer joy, he leapt all together off the ground and clicked his heels, as he had not done since he was a youngster. When the cabby looked at the tip Scrooge gave him upon arriving at his house, he exclaimed in astonishment.

"Blimey, guv, that's a bloody fortune, that is! I think I'll take the missus to the seaside on that!"

As Scrooge knelt to say his prayers before climbing into bed that night – for he had said them regularly ever since that special Christmas – he was all thankfulness and no petition. This was not unusual, for he seldom any more expressed a desire to the divinity but invariably intoned his thanksgivings for the plenitude of his life; but this time his thankfulness was so full that it resembled a fountain of gratitude bubbling up from deep within and cascading down like a waterfall, he was so excited about his prospects for the future now that he had rediscovered Annabelle. He was so atingle as he climbed into bed that he didn't believe he could sleep, yet it was only a minute or two before he had fallen into a deep slumber and dreamed a series of dreams about Annabelle. Sometimes the two of them were young and lithe, as they had been at the beginning, and other times they were old and infirm. But always his heart was suffused with joy and delight, so that he awakened in the morning wondering if what he remembered from the night before could possibly be true or if he had only dreamed it.

Ordinarily, Scrooge didn't eat much breakfast – perhaps a roll and a cup of tea or coffee. But that morning he felt ravenously hungry, as if he had traveled to the other side of the moon and back, and cooked himself a full English breakfast of sausage and bacon, eggs, beans, fried bread, and toast, all of which he downed with a pot of strong hot tea. And as he shaved after breakfast, he didn't see the usual face staring back at him from the mirror, but a different one, younger, fuller, and aglow with the prospects of a new life beyond the good one he had enjoyed the day before.

When he entered the offices of Marley, Scrooge, McDougall, & Cratchit, everyone paused to stare at him, for there was definitely something different about him that morning. Was it the cut of his clothes or the color of his tie? The jauntiness of his walk? The tune he was whistling? Or the wistful look on his face and the little smile that crinkled the folds around his eyes? Perhaps it was all of these, and the indefinable spirit within, that seemed somehow to effuse itself through the very pores of his body. Not even the somber news that greeted him in the person of his nephew Fred McDougall, when Fred entered his office and quietly shut the door behind him, was able to dim this joyous spirit.

"I hate to tell you this," said Fred, "but I've discovered the culprit that's been lifting money from the till."

"Oh?" said Scrooge, only half-interested.

Fred shook his head in sad acknowledgment. "It's Peter."

"Peter? Bob's Peter?"

"Yes. I set a little trap yesterday with some marked bills, then had my secretary keep a sharp watch on the door to see who went in and out when I wasn't there. There were only three people who entered and left. Donald Frierson, the chap who handles delinquent accounts. Estelle Bridges, who works for

Bob, and Peter. I thought I'd eliminate the least likely first, so went directly to Peter, and without volunteering a reason for my action, demanded to see his purse. He was shy about it, but relinquished the purse. One look settled it; three of the missing bills were in it, each marked with my little 'x' in a corner."

"Oh, my."

"We had a long talk. He finally broke down and confessed that he'd needed money several times in recent weeks to settle some gambling debts. He begged me not to tell Bob. Said it would break his heart. I don't know how we can not tell him, do you? What do you advise, Uncle?" Scrooge had a pensive look as he mulled the problem in his head. He liked young Peter. He also agreed that it would break Bob's heart if his crime were to be made public. In the old days, Scrooge knew, he would have felt no mercy. He would have called the police into the office and had the boy arrested at once, and without compunction seen the young man sent to prison and ruined forever.

Now, however, his heart required no such decisive justice. Instead, he felt a kind of pity for the boy; and said to Fred, "Let me handle it, Fred. Ask the lad to come and see me, will you?"

It was a broken child who faced him a few minutes later. The collapsed posture of his body, the obvious fear upon his face, the nervousness in his voice, though he spoke little, all betrayed his great anxiety. "Come in, Peter," said Scrooge firmly but not unkindly. "Close the door, will you? Now sit there. We need to talk." Scrooge did not quibble about what the boy had done; that had already been established. He merely went to the heart of the matter: "You have a problem, my boy. You are not the first to have it, and you will not be the last. But we must take care that it not ruin your life before you are half begun. Now, set your mind at ease, I am not going to tell your father about this. In fact, no one in this firm will know about it but Mr. McDougall, myself, and you. Our concern is not for the money you have taken, although you will be expected to replace that, a little every week until it has all been paid. You could not live with yourself for the next fifty years were we to dismiss the matter without such reparations. What does concern us is this gambling problem I understand you admitted to Mr. McDougall. A thing like that can prove a bitter jockey, my boy, driving you over stiles you were never intended to cross. It can jerk you and whip you and all but destroy your spirit. You don't want that, do you?"

By this time, young Peter was wiping tears with the backs of his hands.

"No, sir," he said timidly.

"Of course you don't!" said Scrooge. "Now here's what you're going to do. First, you are going to avoid the gambling shops like a plague. Do you understand? You are not to go near one. Walk on the other side of the street if you see one ahead, or go around the block another way. You mustn't put yourself in the way of temptation." "Second, you are going to go to church every Sunday and pray to the good Lord to forgive you for having been a gambler and ask his help in overcoming a very wicked habit. I know your father and mother attend services, and I expect you to go with them. I shall ask your father every Monday morning if you were in their company when they went to church on the sabbath day.

"And, third, you are going to repay the money you have taken from the till of this firm until every last penny has been remitted. You will not feel good about yourself if you go do not do this. You can begin this Friday, when you receive your pay packet. Go to Mr. McDougall and hand him an envelope containing this week's payment. Then continue to do this every Friday until your debt is satisfied. Do you understand?"

"Yes, sir." His head was a little higher now.

"And do you agree?"

"Oh, yes, sir. I gladly agree. And thank you, sir."

"Thank me? For what, boy?"

"For not calling the police and sending me to prison, sir. I know I deserved that, but I am glad to have your mercy." "Well," said Scrooge, "there are times in our lives when we all need mercy, and times when we need to extend mercy to others. Don't forget that, son. You too must become a bearer of mercy as you have the opportunity. You'll remember that, won't you?" "Indeed I will, sir," said the lad, his face now shining with hope and confidence again.

"Mr. Scrooge, sir?" he said, looking at last into his employer's eyes.

"Yes, lad?"

Chapter 5

The Detective's Report

"Have you – did you – ever do anything for which you required forgiveness? I mean, as you have now forgiven me?" Scrooge looked into the boy's earnest face and then fell thoughtful for a moment. At last he answered, "Yes, my boy, I did. I truly did. You might even say I was a gambler too. I risked everything to become a wealthy man, and, while some might have judged me a success, I think I failed miserably at achieving what life was intended for. Oh, I made my mark in the world, all right. But it wasn't the right one. I was wrong about money, as I think you have been. Money doesn't make us happy. Not one bit. Happiness – real happiness – comes entirely from other sources. It springs from love and relationships, not material substance. Always remember that, Peter, and you will be a true success in life."

"Thank you, sir," said Peter as he rose to leave the room.

At the door he paused and turned. "I'll never forget this, sir," he said.

"Never!"

Scrooge smiled as the young man left and closed the door behind him. He was pleased for Peter's receptiveness, but also for his own understanding of what he had said. He only wished someone had said those words to him when he was a young man wanting to make his way in life. Now he understood everything so much more clearly.

Later that same morning, Mrs. Cratchit came into Scrooge's office to empty the trash. She apologized for entering while he was at his desk, but he said, "Not at all, my dear. Any time. Any time."

She paused before his desk, her face shining with happiness.

"I don't know what ye said to me Peter, sir" she said, "but it 'elped 'im a treat, it did. 'E's been mopin' around like an ol' bear, but I seen 'im a few minutes ago an' 'e was proper 'appy, 'e was. I said, 'What's come over you, then?', an' 'e said, 'I been talkin' t' Mr. Scrooge, I have, an' 'e made me feel right good about things!' I didn't pry, o' course, but I'm very 'appy 'e's 'is ol' self again, Mr. Scrooge, an' 'e owes it all t' you, sir. You 'ave this mother's gratitude fer whatever it was."

Scrooge smiled. "He's a fine boy, Mrs. Cratchit. He'll be a credit to this firm, you wait and see." He thought of what his life was like before his transformation, and how seldom he had ever felt anything resembling this warm sensation around his heart at having spoken words of encouragement to another. Back then, it was all "Bah, humbug!" but now there was a lovely serenity in his life, as if he were immersed in a hot bath while snow lay deep upon the ground outside.

Mrs. Cratchit had not said all that was on her mind, though. "Mr. Scrooge," she said, "ye'll forgive me if I speak out o' turn, I think, but, y' know, "There's somethin' diff'rent 'bout you today. Somethin' – Well, I don't know what it is, exactly, but there's a kind of glow 'bout y'r face, a radiance, so to speak, as if somethin' good 'ad 'appened to you since the last time I saw you. Somethin' specially good. I don't mean to intrude upon y'r good nature, sir, but I couldn't help observin'."

Scrooge grinned widely, pleased that someone had noticed the uptick in his normally genial nature.

"Bless your heart, Mrs. Cratchit," he said, "there isn't much that escapes your notice, is there?"

She returned his smile and answered, "No, sir, I guess there isn't. My Bob 'e allays says 'e knows 'im inside out, whether 'e's told me what's goin' on in 'is 'eart or not." She paused and then continued: "It's a lady, i'nt it, sir? I'd bet my bottom shillin' on it, that that's what it is. Am I right, sir?"

Scrooge, amazed at her uncanny intuition, smiled more broadly than ever now, then winked to confirm her diagnosis, but said nothing on the subject.

"Oh, I un'erstand," she said. "It's a secret now, i'nt it, Mr. Scrooge? Well, you'll tell us in all good time, I'm sure. I'll just say I'm right glad fer you, Mr. Scrooge. There ain't nothin' as lifts the spirits like a little feelin' o' romance, is there, sir? It's a tonic to us all, I'm sure. You'll excuse me for mentionin' it, I 'ope. There was just somethin' so plain about y'r bearin' that I thought it 'ad to be "love or somethin' in that vicinity. I'm glad t' know I wa'n't wrong." "No, you were not wrong, Mrs. Cratchit," said Scrooge. "In fact, you were very right."

"God bless you, sir," she said, picking up her trash box to go.

"Thank you, Mrs. Cratchit," said Scrooge. "And may God bless you as well."

On Friday evening, Scrooge kept his dinner date with Fred and Nessa McDougall at Chez Dauphin. Nessa wore her new purple dress, which was quite striking on her, and the corsage of white gardenias provided by her thoughtful host. "Thank you, Uncle, for these lovely flowers," she said when she and Fred entered the carriage. "Their aroma is so wonderful that I didn't need to put on any perfume tonight."

Ah, my dear," said Scrooge gallantly, "you are especially beautiful in that dress, and you never need to wear perfume, as sweet as you are." The dinner was excellent. A delicate fois gras to start, filets de sole aux aumandines, pommes de terre de la maison, haricots verts, a fine mixed salad, blue cheese on French bread, and poires au Cointreau with whipped cream and toasted almonds for dessert, with each course accompanied by an appropriate wine.

They talked of many things – how well the business was doing, how satisfying it was to Fred, how often Nessa fussed at him for overworking and not finding time for evenings such as this, what a fine family the Cratchits were, and, the best news of all, that Nessa was expecting a baby and would soon have toretire her purple dress for a while. When news of the baby came out, Scrooge immediately

ordered a bottle of fine champagne and they all toasted the unborn child. "He or she," declared Scrooge, "will have a place for life at Marley, Scrooge, McDougall, & Cratchit!"

"My last time for this until the baby comes," said Nessa, twirling her champagne glass and feeling the bubbles tickling her nose.

Now," said Scrooge at last, "there's something I'd like to ask the two of you. You may have noticed a slight lifting of my spirits these past few days. I'd like to tell you what it's due to. About the time when you were born, Fred, I was seeing a young lady named Annabelle Fezziwig. You've heard me mention old Fezziwig, I'm sure. He was a favorite of mine in those days. There was an understanding for a while that Annabelle and I would marry. But, to my shame, I became so preoccupied with my business interests that I began to neglect this lovely woman, and she wisely broke off our unannounced engagement. Well, I recently had occasion to call upon Miss Fezziwig, or Mrs. Moore, as she is known today, and we had a very amiable reunion. Very amiable, indeed.

"Aha!" said Fred.

Yes. aha," said Scrooge, continuing. "Mrs. Moore's husband died a few years ago, leaving her a widow with two daughters, who are now grown and have gone their own ways, so that she is alone in the fine house her husband left her.

"Aha again!" chimed in Nessa, smiling knowledgeably.

Scrooge smiled back in affirmation. "Now," he said, "the question I want to ask you two, for I trust you in matters of the heart, is this. Would it be foolish of this old codger, who has never married or even paid much attention to women, to court this attractive widow with an eye to marrying her, should she prove amenable to the idea?

Chapter 6

The Reunion

Almost in unison, Fred and Nessa dismissed any notion of hesitance as mere folly. "Of course you should court her," insisted Nessa. "She's single, you're single, you like each other, you find her attractive, you owe it to yourself to marry her, and as soon as possible!

"Hear! Hear!" said Fred, recharging their champagne flutes.

He lifted his glass. "To Missus Moore," he said, "and our dear Uncle Ebenezer!"

Embarrassed slightly, Scrooge joined them in the drink and then thanked them for their opinion, which he said he valued very highly. "You may need to coach me a little from time to time," he said, "as I'm afraid I'm very rusty about these matters."

"It will be our pleasure," said Fred.

"I volunteer to give you excellent advice," said Nessa.

And they all felt especially close to be sharing such an important secret.

Fired on by his conversation with Fred and Nessa, Scrooge lost no time in commencing his courtship of Mrs. Annabelle Moore. He wined her and dined her, sent her flowers, took her candy and books, invited her on picnics and other excursions, walked and rode carriages through the park with her, escorted her to opera and the theater, and generally kept her head awhirl with more attention than she had ever had in her entire life. Finally, after several weeks of intense relations, Annabelle had to call a halt.

"Ebbie," she said, for she always called him that when she had something personal or endearing to confide, "this has got to stop! You are wearing me to a frazzle. I propose that we set a limit on the number of times we see one another in a single week – say once or twice, or three times at the most if there is some very special reason for the third meeting. Why, I have had to begin keeping a special calendar exclusively for our visits. Otherwise, I would offend you by failing to be ready for the theater on an evening when we had agreed to go, or not remembering that it is Sunday and I promised to accompany you to church!" For a moment, Scrooge was halted by this protestation, for he had recently learned that he was not the only man usurping his beloved's time. Once, when he appeared at her door unannounced and had been told by Ginnie she was not at home, he had turned to leave just as a carriage pulled up outside her gate, from which Annabelle emerged in the company of a gentleman he had never seen before. It was obviously a somewhat awkward moment for her as well as Scrooge, but she had bravely introduced her companion, a certain Captain Thomas Q. Twiddle III, a tall person with an erect, military bearing and an astonishingly bold and impressive handlebar mustache. Discomposed by the realization that he was not the only man in his lady's life, and in a brief period of high uncertainty, Scrooge had immediately contacted his old acquaintance Mr. Dooley once more and requested a full report on Captain Twiddle's reputation and situation. In a week's time, Dooley had done his usual discreet job of investigation and returned to Scrooge with a full report, which he happily divulged while smoking another of his employer's fine cigars. A former captain in the imperial army posted to one of the Indian provinces and now a gentleman at leisure, Captain Twiddle, or "Tommy," as he was known to most of his friends and acquaintances, bore a character without stain or blemish. The "Q" in his name, noted Mr. Dooley with a smile, actually stood for "Quumquat," a variant spelling of "kumquat" that occurred when his great grandfather had insisted on naming his newborn son Thomas Quumquat because of his wife's fondness, during her pregnancy, for the small citrus fruit it represented. "This was before the general use of Mr. Johnson's dictionary," suggested Dooley, "in which the proper spelling was first recorded." The nickname the child had borne in his youth, Tommy, apparently stuck to

him, even through military training and service in the army, so that that was how he was now known by most of his acquaintances. Captain Twiddle, it appeared, had never married, although he was frequently espied in the company of this lady or that, sometimes at the theater, other times at a spa, and yet other times strolling through Hyde Park on a Sunday afternoon. Now, faced with Annabelle's declaration that he was requiring too much of her time and energy, Scrooge naturally assumed that she sought to reserve at least part of her attention for the gallant Captain Twiddle, and blurted out, without thinking, "Oh, it's Captain Quumquat is it? Have I been intruding too much upon his schedule?"

Taken aback by this accusation, Annabelle endured a moment of shocked silence. Then she abruptly began to laugh, which discommoded Scrooge to an even greater degree.

"You're jealous!" she said while attempting to curb her laughter.

Confused by her apparently wanton disregard for his serious feelings, Scrooge made a momentary effort at protestation, but only with the result that it produced even more laughter on her part. "Oh, Ebbie," she chortled, "Captain Twiddle's not like that. I mean, yes. I go out occasionally with him, occasionally to a play or a concert. And a few times we've been to dinner together. But -- how shall I put this modestly and with discretion? -- Tommy's not that kind of man. I mean, he's a dear, you know, but he's not exactly a man's man, if you take my meaning. He's a wonderful escort. We've gone out that way together for several years, almost since dear Arthur died. He's every widow's friend. Ask any lady who knows him. We all feel -- safe -- with Tommy. Do you understand?"

Embarrassed at having produced such a tremendous demonstration over such a trifling matter, Scrooge nevertheless felt a great tide of sheer relief pouring through his entire being. The captain -- Tommy -- was no threat at all! Obviously, Annabelle had never once regarded him as a suitor. His own jealousy had been for nothing -- nothing, that is, except to spur him on to a prompter expediency in his quest for the darling Annabelle's hand. Truth be told, it was the reason for his hand now seeking an object within his greatcoat pocket. Years before, when young Ebenezer expected to marry the beautiful Belle, he had bought her a simple gold ring as a token of their engagement. It was not a terribly expensive ring, as he was a mere stocking clerk at the time and could ill afford anything costly; but it was finely crafted and was engraved on the inside with the simple Latin words "Te amo" – "I love you." A jeweler in the next street but one from Fezziwig's business had sold it to him and set it aside while he paid a few shillings a week on it, for he could not pay more. When Annabelle returned it to him, declaring he was too much in love with money to be in love with her, he took it back to the jeweler, hoping to redeem it for the price he had paid. But as the jeweler offered him less than half as much as he had given, he decided to put the ring away and keep it against the unlikely possibility that he might someday meet another woman he would wish to give it to.

The very day after he had first been to visit Mrs. Moore, he had searched it out of the little chest where he kept such paltry valuables, and had ever since had it sitting upon the dresser in his bedroom, where he picked it up, stared at it, and lovingly fondled it at least once or twice a day. Tonight, as he had for several days, he carried it in his pocket, waiting for the arrival of some propitious moment when the stars in the heavens were in the right conjunction and everything conspired to his offering dear Annabelle a proposal of marriage. Now, following her statement of need for a little respite from all the hustle and bustle of the courtship, and her defense of the relationship she had with the generally popular Captain Thomas Q. "Tommy" Twiddle, he knew it was precisely the right time. "I see, my dear," he said, brushing aside all thoughts of a rival suitor. "I too have grown weary of all the comings and goings, the concerts and theaters and visits to museums, the picnics and promenades, the elaborate luncheons and late-night dinners. They have all been a grand pleasure, and I have enjoyed every moment we have spent together. But I too, alas, have been exhausted by trying to match the stride of these events, and often, after behaving like an active young swain when we were together, have returned to my bed at night a crippled old man, worn and bent by the exertions of the day. I have always gone to sleep happy, with a smile on my face, and have slept soundly except for my lovely dreams of you; but I have wakened in the morning as if I had been slaving through the night in some mine or quarry to produce the energy I needed for another day.

"So –"

Here he paused with a bit of drama and was stonily silent as he reached into his pocket for the small parcel he knew was there, withdrew it, and opened it for her to view. Her shock was instantaneous. "Ebbie! Is it what I think it is? I can't believe it! Dear me, my heart is fluttering! It is! The ring! Does it mean what I think it means? Are you – ? Do you – ? Oh, Ebbie!"

Fully delighted by her emotional reaction, Scrooge removed the ring from its old velvet box and gently placed it on her finger. It was a perfect fit!

"I've had it for years," he confessed. "It still bears the inscription it bore all those years ago, professing my love for you. I was such a fool then, to ever take it back. Dear Belle, will you marry me?"

For a moment, she could not speak at all, she was so completely overcome. Then she reached out to draw him close, and planted a big kiss on his cheek. "Of course I will, dear Ebbie," she said. "Of course I will!"

He felt the moisture on his cheek where her tears had touched it.

It was a moment neither of them would ever forget.

Now the days began to rush as Ebenezer and Annabelle's plans were out and more and more people became involved in their feverish round of activities. There were parties and luncheons and dinners galore, and at each they were treated as the royal couple, the romantic Ebenezer and Annabelle, who after an interval of more than thirty years had found their way back together and were now prepared to tie the knot in a way that would give them both security and companionship for the remainder of their lives. If Annabelle had been tired before, she was often bone weary now, but fortunately the new turn of events seemed to imbue her with energy she didn't know she had, so that she could dance till midnight and then be up at seven for a breakfast with friends who wanted to catch up on all the news.

It was the same for Scrooge. If any doubted he would pull his own weight at Marley, Scrooge, McDougall, & Cratchit because of his newly affianced estate, they were quite mistaken, for, like Annabelle, he seemed to have touched some new and deeper vein of vitality that now fed his daily activities with a vigor that surprised even him.

At first they spoke of waiting a year to celebrate their nuptials, as there was so much to do and there were so many legalities to be traversed with their respective attorneys. But one evening they confessed to each other that they could not wait so long to be man and wife. It would be an indescribable torture. And, besides, they were not getting any younger as they waited, as much as they appeared to do so. Annabelle said all right, she thought they should do the deed on New Year's Day. Scrooge said he would agree if she had her heart set on such a symbolic beginning. But, he added, as long as they were moving things up, why not have their wedding at Christmas, for Christmas had been so significant in his own life's history. He had told her by now, of course, about the wondrous evening when the spirits came to call and showed him the absolute error of his ways. "Christmas it is!" she said without delay. "That is a wonderful idea, dear Ebbie. Let us hug and kiss upon it now, and we shall set to work at once to make our fondest dreams come true!"

And so they did.

Annabelle began to assemble her trousseau and Ebenezer began to expedite his own plans for the wedding. He invited the Rev. Mr. Josiah Plumwood and Mrs. Plumwood to dinner at a fine restaurant one night to introduce his fiancee to them, and them to her, for she had already agreed that the marriage should take place in Scrooge's church, St. Martin's in the Swale. That dinner went off beautifully, as both the Plumwoods, and especially Mrs. Plumwood, took immediately to the lovely Annabelle, and Scrooge, beholding the amity between them, did not wait for another time but immediately, before the evening was over, asked Mr. Plumwood if he would do them the honor of conducting their wedding service. He, of course, was delighted, and so it was settled, and the day was entered into the church's calendar.

Chapter 7

Falling in Love Again

I've never done a wedding on Christmas," said Mr. Plumwood. "It sounds like jolly fun, and I shall look forward to it with immense pleasure! Yes, immense indeed!

It was the wedding gift – Scrooge's wedding gift to Annabelle – that now occupied most of his attention. He wanted it to be truly spectacular, something to sweep her off her feet, so to speak. It could never, of course, atone for all the years they had missed because of his abominable greed as a young businessman. But it could, he thought, be so striking, so inimitable, so totally impressive, that it would set a fine tone for their life together now that they were reunited. He considered many alternatives. It might be a trip to Paris. But almost everybody of any means did that, and not only Paris, but Venice and Rome and even Istanbul. What about a journey to the United States, a place he had once thought of visiting as a site for new business ventures? He had heard tales both good and ill of such a trip, some involving long bouts of sea-sickness, and he didn't wish his bride to be made ill by any journey he had planned. A country house, perhaps? That had its appeal. But he and Annabelle were both getting older now, and there were days when his rheumatism bothered him enough to make him think he wouldn't wish to impose the added responsibilities of keeping up yet another home upon either himself or his darling Annabelle. So what should it be?

He knew! The answer sprang full-blown in his head as he was walking to the office. A new house in London! That would be the ticket! He certainly could

Not bring a new bride to live in his own old quarters, which, even if renovated and redecorated by the most skillful crew in the city, would still stand in a neighborhood of houses that had become dilapidated and unattractive. And Annabelle's house, where apparently she assumed they would reside, might prove too small for the kind of life they were now beginning to live, with luncheons and dinner parties and teas with all sorts of friends. No, neither of their present abodes would do, so that settled it in his mind. He would build his bride a new house! And he must set about it at once, for there was precious little time in which to accomplish this dream.

That very day, Scrooge took his partners, Fred McDougall and Bob Cratchit, into his confidence about his scheme, only to have cold water thrown upon it at once. "Uncle," said Fred, "you'll never be able to build a new house in time for your wedding, if you want to present your gift to Annabelle then. It takes months and months to erect a new building, as you should well know."

Bob agreed. "He's right, sir, months and months." "But," protested Scrooge, "we have our own builders, don't we? And we have a lumberyard and a brickyard. Why shouldn't we be able to do it?"

"You might, Mr. Scrooge," said Bob Cratchit, "if you were doing it in the country. But in the city? Here you would have to find a proper bit of land, then secure dozens of building permissions. It could easily take up to a year, even given our extraordinary resources." So Scrooge settled for an alternative, one which was not all that bad once he had given it some thought. If he hadn't time to erect a new house, then he must find an old one, something tasteful and elegant, and refurbish it for his bride. That was what he would do! He would find a great old house and turn it, for all intents and purposes, into a new one. Surely there would be time for that!

"Just," said Fred and Bob, almost simultaneously. "We might barely pull it off if we can get onto it right away."

And so they did.

Almost at once, Scrooge began to scour the most desirable neighborhoods in the city. He looked high and low. For more than a fortnight, he devoted his days to a bevy of realtors who were only too happy to assist him. And in the end they located amongst them a most agreeable townhouse in the area known as Russell Square, not far from the sprawling British Museum, a neighborhood known all over London as one of the finest in the country. Four stories tall, and with an ample basement for the kitchen and servants' quarters, it faced the sun in the afternoon, adding a patina of burnished light to the lovely brick of the building, and it looked out upon the attractive greenery of the ample park before it. The street was wide enough for several carriages to pass at once, and across the square lay the famous Great Russell Hotel, which entertained high-class guests from all over the world wishing to be near the museum and the theater district, the latter being little more than a dozen blocks away.

Scrooge knew as he walked through the house, which was not in bad condition at all, even as it stood, that this was the one. He could envision his Annabelle in the large bedroom on the second floor, the one with an adjacent bath, and could see her descending the broad staircase with the ornate stone banister into the ample receiving hall below. Yes, he thought, it was perfect, even more perfect than any new house he might have erected in any other part of the city. He agreed so readily to buy it, and at the price that was set upon it, that the presiding realtor and his client were very astonished, and wondered if they should not have named a higher price than the one at which it was offered.

Fred himself took an active role in the restoring of the lovely house, though restoration was almost too strong a word for the few things required to turn this home into a castle. There was a minimum of replastering to be done – the moisture in the primary bathroom had loosened some of the old ceiling, so that it needed to be taken down and replaced – and there was minimal repair to some of the floors, particularly the ones that had not been covered in carpet. The entire place was repainted, from top to bottom, for Scrooge wanted it all as fresh as a spring morning when he and Annabelle assumed their occupancy. New tile was installed in the bathrooms, and new equipment in the kitchen. A great, sparkling chandelier was hung in the reception area, so that that large hall said unmistakably, "Welcome to a resplendent house!" And new furniture was required for the entire home – furniture Scrooge obtained at wholesale prices, for Marley, Scrooge, McDougall, & Cratchit owned not only a couple of fine furniture stores, but an entire furniture warehouse that serviced other stores. Scrooge's pride was the enormous banquet table for the dining room, a gorgeous, ornately carved and hand-polished wooden beauty from a showroom in Paris, with gracefully designed chairs all around made more comfortable by cushions covered in Oriental silk brocade. It could easily accommodate twenty-four guests, with room to squeeze in another half dozen should the need arise.

All of this renovation was accomplished in highest secrecy, of course, for Scrooge wished his wedding gift to remain a mystery to his bride until the day they married, when he would escort her in the wedding carriage from the elaborate reception right to the steps of her own new house. Correction: their new house. Annabelle knew he was up to something, of course; wives and would-be-wives, or almost-wives, are difficult to fool. But Scrooge would only tell her that he had many things to occupy his time before they married, and that he knew she would like the gift he was preparing for her. In the meantime, he let her think they would be residing in her old house at 128 1/2 Outer Lane, and didn't even attempt to prevent her having some painting and small repairs accomplished there in preparation for his advent. In fact, he even asked Bob Cratchit to arrange the workmen for her, so that she would not have to scramble on her own to get things done. In the meantime, Scrooge was becoming acquainted with Annabelle's larger family, especially her two lovely daughters, as Annabelle was being introduced to Fred and Nessa, their new baby Nell, Bob and Mrs. Cratchit, and of course the Cratchit children. Annabelle took a particular liking to Tiny Tim, who was now a stalwart lad of twelve, even though he still favored one hip after his bout with polio and continued to employ a crutch as he hopped around the offices. She found him exceptionally bright and thoughtful, and loved the way his keen eyes sparkled when he smiled at her.

"Tim," she said on one occasion, "I wonder if you would do our Mr. Scrooge and myself a great big favor by consenting to be our ring bearer at the wedding?"

Tim, of course, was greatly honored to be thus chosen, and agreed with alacrity. "I couldn't refuse such a beautiful bride as yourself, madam," he replied. "If I did, I would never forgive myself. And, who knows, I might be gettin' married one day myself, and would wish to invite you to my wedding. One interesting development that Scrooge and others thought worth watching was the budding friendship between the Cratchits' son Peter and Mrs. Margaret Hennessy, the younger of Annabelle's two daughters. She was a couple of years older than he, but that seldom matters in the attraction between the sexes, and she seemed to find him not only handsome but hard-working and ambitious. "He's such a nice young man," she said to her mother at tea one day, "he's very polite and kind, and I would judge that he has a great future ahead of him with the firm."

"That he has," said her mother, coyly, not attempting to pry but showing a mature woman's ability to wait and accept tidbits of information as they are offered. "And don't you like his parents? Mrs. Cratchit loves to chatter, I admit, but she has a heart of gold. She and her husband have both been very good to

Ebenezer, and are as near to being family to him as Fred and Nessa themselves."

On learning that Margaret was a widow, Peter asked if he might call on her some time, and she eagerly agreed, suggesting that a Sunday afternoon's stroll in Hyde Park might be nice. "They have a wonderful band concert there, you know," she added, "and I love to sit and listen to the music." At this, Peter not only agreed but admitted to owning a concertina on which he enjoyed playing whenever he had the time, and she let him know at once that it would be her great pleasure to hear him play.

One afternoon, Peter knocked at Scrooge's office door, which was open, and entered when Scrooge invited him to come in.

"I just want to thank you, Mr. Scrooge, for introducing me to Mrs. Hennessy," he said. "We are getting along very well."

"Ah," said Scrooge, "I'm very glad to hear that, my boy. I thought the two of you seemed unusually compatible."

"Oh, we are, sir, we are!" said the lad.

Scrooge had a grin on his face. "What is it, sir?" asked Peter.

"You mean, what am I grinning about? I suppose I was just thinking, son, about your nature."

"My nature, sir?"

Scrooge smiled, careful that the boy should not mistake what he was about to say as criticism. "Your nature – your confession that you have a gambler's blood inside you. I was simply thinking that your relationship with Mrs. Hennessy may well be the biggest gamble you will ever take. It is always that way when a young man falls in love. How it will all turn out is invariably a risk, a very big one. But the good side of that is that the odds are very much in the gambler's favor that everything will turn out well and he will be happier than he has ever been in his life."

The young man smiled shyly. "I understand, sir, and I'm sure you're right. I'm cured of the other kind of gambling, thanks to you, sir. But I don't want to be cured of this kind."

Chapter 8

The Proposal

"Well said," said Scrooge. "I wish you the best!"

"And I you, sir," returned Peter. If Scrooge had been a generous man before, he now became, if possible, even more munificent in his gifts. He was involved with a dozen or more charities around London, including a foundling society, a prison reform group, the education society, the Little Brothers and Sisters of the Poor, the general food warehouse, the hospital fund for the indigent, and the "rents society," whose purpose it was to help people who had fallen in arrears on their rent to make up the money they lacked so they wouldn't be dispossessed from their homes. He continued, of course, to carry a great wad of bank notes in his pockets in order to defray the needs of any he simply happened to encounter in the course of a walk about town or a visit to his church. Bob Cratchit expressed concern about this, for he knew from his own experience that there are people lurking in alleyways and behind carriages who would as soon mug a passerby for his money and his watch as to look at him, and that there were in the course of a single day sometimes as many as forty or fifty needless deaths from such attacks. But people soon knew Ebenezer Scrooge by sight, and apparently, as news of his generosity spread throughout the city, they simply asked him for money when they needed it instead of attacking him to take what was in his pockets. Only one time had Scrooge been jeopardized by his being a man of means, and he did not tell Bob Cratchit about this, preferring to keep it secret. Walking home from the office one dark and foggy night, he had been set upon by a very large man and dragged into an alley, where the man punched him once in the face before ransacking his coat and trousers pockets in search of money. A policeman happened to pass by the mouth of the alley as this altercation was occurring, and, detecting sounds of a scuffle, rushed to Scrooge's aid. The varlet who had stolen his purse and watch fob, however, fled into the deeper darkness beyond the street and was not apprehended at the time. The solicitous policeman assisted Scrooge the few blocks to his house and saw him safely inside, where Scrooge applied some iodine to the cut below his eye and went to bed with gratitude for his narrow escape. The following day, the same policeman arrived at his house to announce that he and a colleague had apprehended the assailant as he was trying to pawn the golden fob from Scrooge's watch, which

had his name upon it because it was awarded to him by one of the many charitable foundations to which he contributed. He wanted Scrooge to accompany him to the court and identify the man in question. Scrooge agreed, although he said it had been very dark and he didn't actually get a good look at the man.

In the court room, he had no doubt in his mind about the assailant, as he could tell from the sheer bulk of the man that he was the one who attacked him the night before. But the man had a simple, honest face, and Scrooge could not believe the man would have set upon him as he did unless it was for some dire and pressing need.

"Mr. Scrooge," said the magistrate, "can you identify this man, Wilfred Tarkington, as the one who cruelly attacked you in an alley off Beale Street last evening and seized your purse and watch fob?"

Scrooge looked again at the defendant, whose face was now so downcast that he felt sorry for him, and replied, "No, your honor, I cannot truthfully say that this was the man." Then where, Tarkington," the magistrate continued, turning to the defendant, "did you obtain the golden watch fob you were attempting to place in pawn at the Hard Times Pawn and Trinket Shop just after the owner opened it this morning? The defendant said nothing, but bowed his head.

"Perhaps, your honor," ventured Scrooge, "he found it in the alley. There was a scuffle, you see, and it might well have fallen to the ground, where this kind of item is and I simply did not see it in the darkness."

"Is that the way it was?" the magistrate asked, turning toward Tarkington.

Again, Tarkington stood mute, his chin lowered in humiliation.

"Your honor," interrupted Scrooge again, "I think I know this man, and do not believe him guilty of such a crime. I will venture to take him into my charge, if you will allow it, and stand good for his character today and in the future."

The magistrate regarded Tarkington. "Sir," he said, "you have heard what Mr. Scrooge has said. He is an upstanding citizen. I have seen his name in the newspapers many times. If he vouches for you, then I must regard his word and release you into his care and supervision. The case is dismissed."

In the street outside the court house, the man stood meekly in front of his benefactor. "I - I do not know what to say, sir, for it was I who took your purse."

"I know," said Scrooge. "But you are not the sort of man who does this as a habit, Mr. Tarkington. I know men, and you are not that kind of man. Why don't you join me for a roll and coffee at that coffee house over there and we'll talk about your situation." Over coffee and rolls, Scrooge learned that the man, who was known to all his friends as simply Wilf, was in a panic because his wife was ill and needed treatment from a specialist, though he had not the means to pay for it. He had quit his work as a cabby some two months earlier to attend his ailing wife and their children, and all his funds had been exhausted. Half mad with anxiety and desperation, he had fired up his courage with two glasses of ale and set out from the pub to find a rich toff and relieve him of his wallet. Tears coursed down his rough cheeks as he talked about his wife and the operation she needed, and about his little children who needed their mother, and Scrooge was deeply touched.

They had ended by Scrooge's taking Wilf back to the office with him and introducing him to Bob Cratchit with the recommendation that Bob find him a job as a driver for one of the company's many lorries. He advanced him a month's wages out of his own pocket, and gave Wilf the name of his own doctor in Harley Street, with instructions to carry his wife to the doctor's offices and have her treated at Scrooge's expense. Often, taking pity on some man or woman who was out of work and desperate for help, Scrooge would bring the person to Fred or Bob and ask if they wouldn't find some work for the person to do, and almost always they managed to find some spot where the man or woman could be most useful, even if it was only as a laborer in one of the brickyards or cement plants the company owned. Bob, with his background in accountancy, sometimes expressed the worry to Fred that Mr. Scrooge was going to spend the company itself into the poorhouse, but ironically the profits of the business seemed to float like a ship on the tide of whatever monies its principle owner expended in the course of his charitable work. The thing about Scrooge, as almost everybody who knew this more recent incarnation of him could testify, was that he didn't merely see the poor around him as objects of pity or compassion, but genuinely viewed them as persons, as sensitive, fully developed human beings in need of temporary assistance. Helping them, he was convinced, was all most of them required to turn their backs on dependency and become self-supporting citizens once more. It was hard, from the evidence, to gainsay this philosophy, for indeed many of those to whom he extended a helping hand ended by becoming contributing members of society and reaching out to others in return for the good will shown to them.

Scrooge and his rector, the Rev. Mr. Josiah Plumwood, had numerous discussions on this subject, because Mr. Plumwood, for all his charitable nature, had a far more saturnine opinion of human nature than his church's generous benefactor. Plumwood would say, for example, "Mr. Scrooge, my friend, it makes me very happy to watch the way you reach out with all your soul to help those around you, but it also worries me, for I believe that many take advantage of your good nature instead of solving their own problems as they ought to do." Scrooge would say, in return, "Now Mr. Plumwood, my dear fellow, I'm afraid you are a Calvinist when it comes to people. You speak of a generous, forgiving deity but

ironically the profits of the business seemed to float like a ship on the tide of whatever monies its principle owner expended in the course of his charitable work. The thing about Scrooge, as almost everybody who knew this more recent incarnation of him could testify, was that he didn't merely see the poor around him as objects of pity or compassion, but genuinely viewed them as persons, as sensitive, fully developed human beings in need of temporary assistance. Helping them, he was convinced, was all most of them required to turn their backs on dependency and become self-supporting citizens once more. It was hard, from the evidence, to gainsay this philosophy, for indeed many of those to whom he extended a helping hand ended by becoming contributing members of society and reaching out to others in return for the good will shown to them.

Scrooge and his rector, the Rev. Mr. Josiah Plumwood, had numerous discussions on this subject, because Mr. Plumwood, for all his charitable nature, had a far more saturnine opinion of human nature than his church's generous benefactor. Plumwood would say, for example, "Mr. Scrooge, my friend, it makes me very happy to watch the way you reach out with all your soul to help those around you, but it also worries me, for I believe that many take advantage of your good nature instead of solving their own problems as they ought to do." Scrooge would say, in return, "Now Mr. Plumwood, my dear fellow, I'm afraid you are a Calvinist when it comes to people. You speak of a generous, forgiving deity but espouse a theology that is decidedly negative in its outlook on the human soul. I myself am more of an Arminian, I think, and am convinced that the average person, given half a chance, will do good and not evil to his fellows, and wishes to be an honest, hard-working, useful member of society." And so it would go, up and down the oak tree and all around the Maypole, but their discussions were always light and easy and of a philosophical nature, so that as much as they disagreed they never fell out in spirit, but continued always in a bond of brotherly love. Mrs. Plumwood, for her part, often agreed with Scrooge and not with her husband, chiding her husband for his "dark opinion of every situation" and the "preachery" tone he adopted in his sermons from the pulpit, although he rarely sounded so in other situations. Scrooge would laugh and tease them that they were mismatched, and then he would say that they were Yea and Nay; Ying and Yang, the mirror opposites of one another and therefore a wonderfully complementary pair! As late summer gave way to fall, the work on the house at 79 Russell Square continued apace, and it was Scrooge's pleasure, at some time each day, to slip away from the office and take a cab to the Great Russell Hotel, where he would enjoy a cup of coffee before strolling across the pleasant green to view the progress of the work crew. Often he would compliment the sanders or painters or plasterers, and, if he thought any of them to be in want of any kind, would generally get them alone on some pretext and slip them ten or twenty pounds to help them out. Thus he won the deep respect and admiration of them all, who looked upon him, not as some eccentric millionaire with no right to the blessings he enjoyed, but as a true aristocrat among men, a gentleman whose heart was boundless and whose generosity was beyond compare.

Only rarely did he offer a comment to the effect that he preferred something done another way from that in which it had been done, for he was mostly an admirer who had come to wander about, savoring the beauty and enjoyment of a life he could already anticipate within the lovely dwelling.

Sometimes, at the conclusion of his tour, he would stop at the hotel for lunch, or else take a cab to Piccadilly and eat in one of his favorite restaurants there. Once, when he was dining at the Great Russell, he was startled to look up and see his fiancée, Mrs. Moore, entering with two lady friends he had not met before. Obviously they had come to enjoy lunch and gossip about whatever it is that women talk about on such occasions, and, as they did not see him, he quietly paid his bill, tipped the waiter, and attempted to slip out of the room, though not before Annabelle had spotted him and told her waiter to catch him and bring him to her table. He feigned a great surprise as he approached, and said what a shock it was to see her there, of all places, for he had been in the area to call on a businessman and had simply chanced to see the hotel and inquired if they had a restaurant on the premises. Did she come there often? he asked, quite innocently.

No, it was only the second time she had ever been there. One of her friends had expressed a desire to dine there because of the tasty shepherd's pie she knew they served, and so the three of them had made a party to come together.

Scrooge made a resolution to be more careful in the future, for if she found him there again she might begin to suspect something, or, worse yet, might actually see him entering or leaving the house at 79 Russell Square. But if she did, he reminded himself, he need only explain that some of his crews were working there and it had been necessary for him to seek a workman out because a relative of the workman had suffered an emergency and needed him to come.

Generally, he had made a point of honesty and eschewed a lie, but in a case like this he believed it quite allowable to stretch a point or cover his tracks with a minor deceit in order to spare his loved one an early realization of what he was about in her behalf.

Later in the week, when he was visiting Jacob Marley's grave and bringing Jacob up to date on all that had transpired since his last attendance, Scrooge narrated for his old friend and partner this narrow escape when he had encountered Annabelle in the vicinity of the house he was preparing for their marriage day.

"I could almost wish she had found out," he mused after describing the near discovery, "for then I could cease pretending I was busy running this errand or that to be away from the office and we could enjoy these little visits to the house together. But I suppose it's best this way. I've wanted it to be a secret, and it is only another three months before the work will be complete and she and I will view the house together as man and wife, and then I shall be able to enjoy her great surprise at what has been accomplished without her knowledge."

He told Jacob of all that was happening in the business, how they seemed to expand indefinitely by purchasing this warehouse and that foundry, or this supply house and that factory.

"Oh, Jacob," he exclaimed at one point, "it is almost magical, what has happened to me since that fateful Christmas eve when you visited me in your awful chains and warned me of the spirits' visits. So many wonderful things have transpired, and often I reflect that in some indefinable way I owe them all to you. Dear Jacob, I hope the good I have tried to do since that wondrous evening has served to reduce the size of all the chains being forged for me, and even more to eliminate yours entirely. For you have a part in every thing I do, you know. If it had not been for you and your good offices, I should be now in my grave and suffering the pains of an everlasting hell. As it is, I have never known such heaven! And soon, when I have married my Annabelle, my bliss will be unspeakable, for I shall be whole as I have never been in all my days. My heart is fairly bursting, old friend. I do wish you could be at our wedding. I would have you at my side as my best man, you know. But you will be there in spirit, I am confident, and I shall expect to see you smiling down on me from some aerie in the church, perhaps from atop the organ pipes or some small balcony in an apse. I have asked my nephew Fred to stand as my best man, and he was glad enough to do it. But there will be sufficient room between us for your nimble incubus, and I shall sense your presence whether my eyes can see you there or not. The very angels in heaven will sing out when we are pronounced man and wife, Jacob, and I am sure that God will note your being there! As the workmen completed their tasks at 79 Russell Square, Scrooge invited Mrs. Cratchit to accompany him there and review the situation to offer any advice she might have about what still needed to be done, and she was only too happy to oblige. The two of them rambled through the house together, floor by floor, as she admired the beauty of the place, the handsomeness of the woodwork and the furnishings, and the sheer spaciousness of the rooms.

"My, my, Mr. Scrooge," she sighed, "it be a palace, or I 'as never seen one! You 'ave outdone yourself on this one, sir, or I am no judge at all."

Chapter 9

Wedding Plans

"Thank you, Mrs. Cratchit," said Scrooge, "I am very happy that you approve. But are there other things that require to be done, do you think, little things, perhaps, that the workmen have overlooked and you, as a lady of taste, can see will need attention before we're through?"

Trying to focus from her overall admiration of the magnificent home to the minuter aspects of the dwelling and its furnishings, she began to tick off a list of little things that she, as a woman, would wish to change or rectify if she were the mistress of the household. There were some recent scuff marks on the wall up the stairway that needed to be painted over and some tiny scars on the floor of a sitting room, made, she surmised, by the moving of a highboy that stood but a few inches from the marks. The water pressure in the lavatory of the mistress's bathroom was much too low, she commented,

suggesting a blocked pipe at some place along the water's route. The damper in the fireplace of the master's bedroom did not close properly, permitting a draft of cold air in the winter time.

There was paint on a few of the windows where some careless workman had not cleaned up sufficiently after painting the window frames. And one of the windows in the living room was stuck, suggesting the need for a new sash or some trimming of the window frame itself. But overall, she said, the men had done a first-rate job and any woman would be an ingrate to carp about their few mistakes or oversights in the face of such an outstanding and beautiful residence.

"Why," she exclaimed, "th' Queen 'erself, bless 'er, Mr. Scrooge, could not complain of 'avin' t' live in a place as grand as this!"

Scrooge thanked her and asked if she could think of anything else he might have overlooked.

"Well, sir," she responded, after a moment's consideration, "you 'ave prob'bly already planned for this, but what about staffin'?"

"Staffing?" echoed Scrooge. "Yes, sir. I means, some people t' help look after this grand house an' all. A cook an' cook's maid fer that beautiful kitchen down there, an' a lady's maid fer ver wife, sir, an' a valet fer yourself. An' a butler, o' course, t' look after ever thin'. Ever' big house I knows 'as a butler."

Scrooge, who had always lived frugally and never employed any kind of personal servant in his own home, except for a girl who came in for a few hours once a week to clean and tidy up, do the washing, and change the linens, had not given a single thought to the staffing of such a great house as the one to which he planned to bring his bride on their wedding day. What was the matter with him?! Where was his mind in all of this?!

"Oh, Mrs. Cratchit," he said, quite flabbergasted, "I'm so glad you mentioned this. I don't know what I was thinking. I wasn't, clearly. I was so caught up in the beauty of the house itself that I hadn't given a single thought to who would manage the house and take care of all the cleaning and cooking. Of course, you are quite right! I shall have to attend to all of these things before bringing Annabelle here."

She patted her employer's arm. "Never you mind, sir," she comforted him. "They's plenty a time left. I'll be glad t' see to it m'self, sir, iffen it's any 'elp to you."

Scrooge looked greatly relieved. "Would you, Mrs. Cratchit? Would you, please? I'd be ever so grateful if you would. I'm sure you know far more of these matters than I do, old curmudgeon that I am. I expect my wife-to-be will bring her own domestic along. And I do know who I'd like as my valet, if I am to have one. I know, that is, if he'd be willing, and if you and Bob approved as well."

She looked at him inquiringly.

"I'm thinking of young Tim," he said. "I know he's young, but he's a fine lad, and very quick to catch on to things. He and I could learn together, and it would give him a trade, so to speak, for the rest of his life." "Mr. Scrooge," she said, a look of awe and wonderment on her face, "that'd be wonderful, sir! My little Timmy, a valet! 'E'd be so honored, I know, sir, an' Bob an' me would be so grateful t' you, sir. An' 'e'd live in this grand 'ouse with you, an' take care o' y'r clothes an' all, sir. Oh, 'e'll be so pleased, an' so will we!"

"Then that's taken care of," said Scrooge, "and very satisfactorily from my point of view."

Suddenly a look of discovery graced Scrooge's face, so that it fairly shone. "I just realized, Mrs. Cratchit," he said with some excitement. "We'll need a driver, won't we? I mean, there's a carriage house behind, and a place for horses and a carriage. Anybody who lives in a house like this is more or less obligated to employ a groom and a driver, am I right?"

"Well," said Mrs. Cratchit. "I 'spect so, sir."

"I know just the man," said Scrooge ecstatically. "He used to be a cabby, before his wife took ill. He works for us at one of our factories. Name's Wilf Tarkington. A huge man, and I'm sure he'd be great with horses. He and his family could occupy the carriage house. His wife could help in the big house, and he and the children could look after the horses!" So life at 79 Russell Square began to take a new shape, a fuller shape, as he and Mrs. Cratchit assumed the work of acquiring a staff to manage the place.

Scrooge had to make some peace with his conscience about having a staff of servants, as he had never employed such personnel before and was not sure it was right that any human being should live in service to another. But eventually he justified the decision by realizing what a convenient arrangement it was within which a man could bestow his patronage and gifts upon others. Thus he satisfied his conscience and invented new avenues through which to share the abundance of his situation. The big house at 79 Russell Square, he determined, would contain one of the happiest households in all of London, and perhaps in all the world!

The renovations on the house were finished in early December, and Mrs. Cratchit took a couple of girls from the office and went over to give it a final "turning out," as she put it. "Y' know, Mr. Scrooge, makin' sure ever'thing's okay fer the missus an' you when ye move in. Don't want no fingerprints on that nice table top or nothin'. Won't take us no time atall, I warrant. But we'll see to it proper like, an' you i'nt got nothin' at all to worry 'bout, as I 'spect they's plenty on y'r mind as it is. Scrooge thanked her and made a mental note to be sure she got something very special in her bonus envelope on the day of the Christmas party:

He himself had one more item on his list about the house, and he had saved it till last. That was to have the great old door knocker on his present dwelling removed and reinstalled on the door at number 79 Russell Square. He owed much to that knocker, he thought, and he wasn't about to leave it behind. It might look like a lion's head most of the time, but he recollected a few moment when to him, at least, it looked like his dear partner, Jacob Marley, and Marley must have a prominent part in the new house.

When he asked Fred which of their workers would be best for such a job, Fred replied that he'd heard the new man, Wilf Tarkington, was very good with his hands, so Scrooge asked him and Wilf said, "O' course, Mr. Scrooge, sir. I'd be happy to!"

"Good," said Scrooge, "because there's something there I'd like to show you, Wilf."

"I'll drive you there myself, Mr. Scrooge, if you don't mind riding on a delivery wagon," said Wilf. "We can take the one I usually drive."

Thus, when Wilf had completed the installation of the heavy knocker and Scrooge had polished it off with his pocket handkerchief, Scrooge said, "Now, let's go around back, Wilf, and see what you think of a proposition I'm about to make you."

They visited the stable house behind the house, and Scrooge led him upstairs to the apartment overhead.

"This is very nice, Mr. Scrooge," said Wilf. "Very nice indeed. Somebody will be very comfy here." "I wondered, Wilf," said Scrooge, "if you and your family would do me the honor of occupying it. I need someone to drive the carriage I intend to get – you know, just around town, chauffeuring my new wife where she needs to go, maybe a trip to the theater or the opera once a week or so, and to church on Sundays. Would you be interested, Wilf?

Chapter 10

The Wedding Gift

"You mean live here and handle your horses?" the big man asked in astonishment.

"That's right."

A smile as big as all outdoors spread over Wilf's huge countenance. "I can't believe it!" he said. "A chance to drive a proper carriage again! And to raise our chilluns in a place like this! Oh, Mr. Scrooge, if I could, I'd pay you for an opportunity like this!"

Scrooge was pleased at this show of warm emotion.

"No, Wilf," he said, "I'll pay you, double whatever you're getting where you are. And we'll get you a uniform, and boots, and a cap, and whatever else goes with such a job. And your wife can help with the work in the house, if she's able and willing, and your children can help you with the horses. They'll all be

paid as well, of course. You'll be like part of our family, living just out here, and it will be our pleasure to see you and your family every day." All of that agreed, the two of them got back in the company wagon and Scrooge directed Wilf to take them to a carriage shop he had seen a few streets away, where they ordered one of the finest carriages the dealer had on offer. It was a large black landau with heavy-duty springs and leather-covered seats, both inside and for the driver. Scrooge loved the smell of it, for the inside was strongly redolent of the leather polish used to put such a patina upon the cushions and the leather linings of the doors.

"That'll look right smart with a coupla dapple grays in front of it, sir," said the salesman, a Mr. Roth. "I know you'd be pleased with it."

"We'll take it," said Scrooge. "And perhaps you can direct us to a good stable where we can find those dapple grays for sale."

At the stable, Wilf's expertise in horses came in handy as he examined their hooves and mouths, then walked the most likely ones around the yard and asked knowledgeable questions of the salesman. Satisfied he had identified the best team in the place, he recommended them to Mr. Scrooge, who instantly approved the choice.

Thus the stage was set for the wedding day, and Scrooge was prepared to surprise his bride, not only with an elegant townhouse in the finest part of London but with a carriage and team worthy of nobility, plus a driver whose very size would intimidate other drivers and whose loyalty to his employer was deepening with every passing day.

The big Christmas party at Marley, Scrooge, McDougall, & Cratchit that year was extraordinary by any measure. It took place on Saturday afternoon and evening before Christmas Day on Sunday and Boxing Day on Monday, which meant a long weekend holiday for all the company's workers, and the upcoming nuptials for Annabelle and Ebenezer charged the air with an excitement as palpable as any of those present had ever felt. The decorations in the company hall were especially festive. Presiding over everything else was an immense Christmas tree – Bob Cratchit said it was almost forty feet tall, and it bore a tinsel star on top that was at least thirty inches in breadth. Ever the accountant, Bob reported that the tree was decked with 475 feet of tinseled rope, 320 glass balls, each four inches in diameter, and 410 candles. It took a team of ten men, many of them working on long ladders, more than thirty minutes to light all the candles, and when they had finished their task, the room glowed with enough warm candlelight to light up even the darkest of hearts!

An orchestra of 54 people, including 8 violinists, 6 trumpeters, 8 French hornists, 9 fifers, 10 bell ringers, and 6 drummers, all led by the director of the Royal Guards Band himself in all his fine regalia, filled the air with spirited music, playing hymns and carols, reels and roundabouts, from five in the evening until almost midnight. An army of caterers worked slavishly to supply food to 12 large tables spread around the rear of the hall, and 16 bartenders served tirelessly to keep the grog and ale flowing freely through the evening. A company of 24 young ladies circulated about the edges of the hall, offering tea and coffee as people desired them, and lifting the spirits of all the attendants by alternately flirting with the men and sympathizing with the women.

The Lord Mayor of London himself was in attendance, as were 16 councilmen, 3 members of the royal family, several peers of the realm, a number of judges and magistrates, and, at someone's count, 17 members of the clergy, including both Church of England and Roman Catholic prelates, an African bishop, and 4 prominent Protestant pulpiteers. Someone said afterward that he had shaken hands with the Rev. Dr. Charles Haddon Spurgeon, the well known pastor of London's popular Metropolitan Tabernacle, and Fred reported that he had been introduced to Charles Dickens, the famous novelist, who had just returned from a triumphant tour of America. All in all, it was the most gala event in all London, and many people had come, not only to dance or make merry, but to see and be seen.

Scrooge and Annabelle were half an hour late in arriving, a consequence, as Scrooge was already learning, of married or almost-married life and the inevitable delays in a woman's preparations for an important outing such as this.

There were, of course, the obligations of her toilette – the makeup and the last minute adjustments to her coiffure – plus of course the lacing of her corset, putting on her shoes, final attentions to her gown, and the general fuss over her clothing as she entered a carriage, lest all the care taken in pressing the gown be nullified by the way it was gathered about her for the journey.

Tim Cratchit, handsome in his new suit for the next day's wedding, though still using his favorite old crutch, which was anything but chic, stood near the door as one of the greeters, and, upon spotting Scrooge and his fiancee alighting from their carriage, signaled to his brother Peter, who in turn nodded to the leader of the orchestra, so that when Scrooge and Annabelle entered there was a mighty fanfare of welcome and the entire crowd, which was huge indeed, turned to applaud the best known benefactor in all of London. No sooner had the two of them doffed their outer garments, handed off to waiting attendants, than they took their place at the head of the line that was forming for a reel, and soon they were dancing away with all the joie de vivre of the gay young couple they had once been in Mr. Fezziwig's ballroom! Then, exhausted by their heroic efforts, they retired, panting and gasping for breath, to the refreshments area, where they shook hands, exchanged hugs, and joined in the banter of their many friends and admirers. Everyone knew, of course, that two days later would be their wedding day, and so they were the target of manifold good wishes and God-bless-yous on every side.

Annabelle's children, Celia and Margaret, were both in attendance, Celia with her handsome husband Delbert Newsome Crane, and Margaret on the arm of Peter Cratchit, looking as natural there as any eager young woman at the side of her beau. Scrooge noticed Peter especially, and predicted to Annabelle, "I know another couple who will soon be making their marriage announcement, or I am no judge of human behavior!"

The evening flowed by like a massive river, bearing all before it in its grand entourage. Soon the exertions of the jigs and reels began to show in the countenances of the dancers, especially in the women, whose coiffures had relaxed, allowing wisps of hair to droop about their faces, and whose dresses, in more instances than not, had shifted in the activities, so that they hung sometimes more to the left and other times more to the right. But an air of general happiness prevailed, and, as faces became flushed from the dancing and drinking, all seemed to know that this was the ball of the season and they weren't likely ever to see another quite like it. This awareness itself added to the overall satisfaction of the attendees, and many were overheard to say, as they eventually donned their wraps and exited to their carriages, that this was the finest and most exciting event they had ever attended. There were a few elderly folk who had been present for the coronation parties for Queen Victoria, and even they agreed that those marvelous events, for all their excitement and royalty, were neither so convivial nor so downright pleasurable as this one.

"Oh, Ebbie," murmured Annabelle as Scrooge helped her down from their carriage and escorted her to the door of her house in Outer Lane, "I never believed I could be as happy as this! How can I ever thank you for coming back into my life?"

"Belle," he replied, holding her hands in his and looking into her sparkling blue eyes, made even more entrancing by a nearby gaslight, "it is I who have to thank you. You have revived this old heart as nothing else could have done, and given me more joy than I ever imagined possible in this life. I can hardly wait until Christmas day, when you will become my wife after all these many years!" If Annabelle's thoughts were of the next day as she hung up her dress and made ready for bed, expecting that on that night she and Scrooge would be spending their first night together in this very room. Scrooge's, as Wilf drove him back home, were of the big surprise he had in store for her, and the wonderful house at 79 Russell Square where they would spend not only their first night of wedded bliss but the remainder of their years together. With a sense of boyish playfulness, he had decided to have their wedding reception, not at a restaurant near to St. Martin's in the Swale, where they would be married, but at the stylish Great Russell Hotel, across the wide green from their new abode, and to keep the house a secret from Annabelle until they emerged from the reception, she thinking they would take a long carriage ride to her old house and he knowing it would be a very short ride indeed, a brief trot around the block and over to number 79!

Scrooge had asked Fred and Bob to see that many of the flowers that adorned the great hall for their Christmas party on Saturday evening should be borne with care to St. Martin's Church, where they would create a festive environment for the morning services and then a lovely, perfumed ambiance for the wedding in the afternoon. But one particularly large and sumptuous bouquet he had requisitioned for himself, and asked Wilf Tarkington to carry him and it to the cemetery early on Sunday morning, where they set it at the base of Jacob Marley's handsome mausoleum. Then Wilf discreetly retreated to wait at the carriage as Scrooge sat on his stone bench to commune for a few minutes with the spirit of his late partner. Well, Jacob," Scrooge began, "this is it, old friend! Today your unworthy partner will be married to the girl of his dreams – the only one he ever dreamed about. You know her well, of course, for she is old Fezziwig's daughter. And Jacob, she is all the more beautiful today for the many years that have passed since you and I had such wonderful times at Fezziwig's parties. Not quite as slender, of course, and her hair has turned silver. But the elegance, the air of saintly beauty, is still there, and more refined and voluminous than ever. You know all of this, of course, and remember that I said I shall expect your presence at the service. That is one of the things I have discovered about growing older, Jacob. One has this tremendous urge to gather to oneself all the souls one has ever known and loved, to bind us all together in one great soul, one overarching spirit of love and unity. You understand what I am so poorly trying to express, of course, for you have a vantage point from which to know all the things I have yet to learn.

"These flowers," he said a few moments later, gesturing at the grand bouquet, "are from our big party last night, though of course you knew that already, didn't you, my friend? I wanted them to be here where you could see them and others could behold the warm regard in which you are still held by one who cared for you as if you were a brother."

Reviewing his mind a bit further, he remarked, "Oh, by the way, Jacob, you remember the Cratchit lad, I'm sure, little Tiny Tim. Well, Tim's growing into a fine young man, and is very good with responsibility. He'll be the ring bearer at our wedding this afternoon. It was Belle's wish that he do it, even though he's getting a mite old for such things. And he will be my new valet in the home we're moving into. I thought you'd want to hear about him."

"Well," he at last concluded, "it is time for me to get on to church. I mustn't miss the worship at eleven, although I gave Belle leave not to accompany me today, knowing she would need extra rest today and time to compose herself before the fateful event this afternoon. So I'll say goodbye for now, old friend, and see you at my wedding."

If there was a huge turnout at Saturday's party, there was a somewhat smaller but equally excited crowd at St. Martin's in the Swale on Sunday afternoon for the wedding of Mrs. Annabelle Moore and Mr. Ebenezer Scrooge, whose bans had been read and posted on the church bulletin board several weeks before. Many came early to be sure of acquiring a seat, and by the time Scrooge arrived, a little after

three-thirty, the place was filled, with a considerable crowd of spectators waiting outside the church, spilling from the churchyard onto the sidewalks and even in the street beyond. Fred McDougall, who was to serve as best man, had collected him from his home so that Wilf Tarkington could fetch Annabelle and her family in the fancy carriage, and the two of them made their way together through the crowds of well-wishers.

Chapter 11

Building the House

In the sacristy, they found Nessa McDougall and the Cratchits, all in their finest clothes and eager to get on with the ceremony. Peter, who was one of the ushers, was the only Cratchit missing, and the others, Bob, Mrs. Cratchit, and the remaining children, had been shined and polished into beaming angels. "Ah, Mr. Scrooge," said Mrs. Cratchit, "ye're a sight fer sore eyes, ye are, wi' y'r lovely tuxedo an' that white bow tie. All ye needs now is this flower in y'r button'ole." And she proceeded to affix the carnation where it showed to the best effect. "Now," she pronounced, stepping back and sighing with deep inner satisfaction, "ye're perfect, sir, absolutely perfect!"

"Thank you, Mrs. Cratchit," he rejoined, "and thank you all for being here to support me. This is the finest hour of my life, I do declare, and I am happy to be surrounded by such good friends." Presently, young Tim, who kept peering through a partially opened door for a signal from Peter, saw what he was waiting for, and announced, "They're here, Mr. Scrooge, they're here! They're waiting in the narthex, sir. Soon, the venerable old organist was playing Pachelbel's "Canon in D Major" on the venerable old organ, which was the agreed-upon cue for Scrooge and Fred to take their places at the front of the church. Then the "Canon" was ended and in its place sounded the ancient strains of the Wedding March itself. First came Tim, bearing a rich velvet pillow to which the golden rings were attached by light ribbons. Scrooge and Fred stood looking to the rear of the sanctuary to behold the sight of Annabelle, accoutered in her flowing white dress, proceeding through the double door and onto the aisle that led to the altar. She paused a moment as one of her daughters – Scrooge thought it was Celia – adjusted the train of her dress, and then she was drawing nearer by the moment. They had talked about having her handsome son-in-law, Delbert Newsome Crane, escort her to the altar, and Scrooge had suggested that they employ Captain Tommy in this capacity, as he thought it would show his magnanimity toward one he had first suspected was himself a rival for Annabelle's hand. But she had been the one to say, in the end, "No, this is my decision, Ebbie, as it was my decision to marry you, and I wish to come to you on my own, not on the arm of another man." And so it was that she came down the aisle alone, a vision of loveliness floating among invisible clouds. She had worried about wearing white, as this was not her first marital experience, but Scrooge was the one who cast the deciding vote on that issue, arguing that in a sense she had always been his love and that entitled her to arrive at the front in the color most associated with virginal affection. The Rev. Mr. Plumwood, who had a fine speaking voice honed by long experience in the chancel, read the traditional service from the Book of Common Prayer, the one beginning, "Dearly beloved, we are gathered together here in the sight of God, and in the face of this company, to join together this Man and this Woman in holy Matrimony," and ending, "I pronounce that they are Man and Wife. In the Name of the Father, and of the Son and of the Holy Ghost. Amen."

The entire ceremony took little more than ten minutes, even with Rev. Plumwood's slow, sonorous way of speaking, and soon the newly united couple were emerging from the church doors under showers of rice and flowers and standing before the gates of the churchyard, which by a quaint tradition the children had laced together with ribbons and would stand behind until the groom tossed a pocketful of coins through the bars to them, thereby inducing them to cut the ribbons and allow the married couple to proceed.

Many people, especially Nessa and Mrs. Cratchit and Annabelle's daughters, shed tears of happiness for the beauty of a wedding, but there was not a drop of sentimentality to be viewed on Scrooge's face, or, for that matter, on his bride's. They were both radiant with joy and eagerness, and looked much younger than their actual years, for each felt that at last their lives had been joined as they were meant to be all those decades ago. There were old boots and buckets and spoons affixed to the back of the beautiful carriage, which had been decorated with an enormous white ribbon, and these clattered amiably as Wilf told the horses to "Walk on," and they commenced their journey to the Great Russell Hotel. All along the way, people waved, blew kisses, and shouted merry Christmas and best wishes, pleased and amazed, perhaps, to see a couple as old as they newly married and grasping life by the hilt to live it bravely and happily for however many years were left to them.

As they had a head start on the crowd, Wilf elected to drive them through Hyde Park for a few minutes before heading for Russell Square, so that the wedding guests would have time to arrive before the bride and groom. As they drove by the pavilion where the band was giving a special holiday concert, this time consisting of familiar carols, the director spied their carriage, surmised its mission, and abruptly called for his band to cease the number it was playing and switch to a peppy version of Wagner's bridal chorus, popularly known as "Here Comes the Bride," which caused the entire crowd to turn, stand, and generously applaud the lucky couple. When they did finally arrive at the hotel, the ballroom was crowded with well wishers who had already commenced to enjoy the champagne and hors d'oeuvres, so that there was an air of joyous festivity already afoot as they swept into the room. The ensemble assigned to provide chamber music for the reception likewise struck up "Here Comes the Bride," and everybody clapped vigorously and shouted out their approbation. Soon Scrooge and Annabelle were whirling gracefully around the dance floor to the strains of the "Christmas Waltz," and then many others were joining them, so that it wasn't long before the floor was too crowded for easy movement and some began to drift away to the refreshment tables and the chairs surrounding the dance area.

The wedding cake was huge – Margaret Hennessy estimated it at six feet tall, but Mrs. Cratchit, who had been in charge of arrangements, corrected her, giving its exact dimensions as seven and a half feet in height, with a base whose diameter was four and a half feet, and there was great fascination with it as Annabelle signaled that she was ready to serve her new husband with the first slice. The women all marveled at the beauty of the decorative icing, saying they could not imagine anyone's having produced such a work of culinary art, and the menfolk all said, "That looks good enough to eat!"

A number of toasts were offered to the bride and groom, and a small army of waiters circulated among the guests, filling up glasses as the toasts proceeded. Irishmen offered Irish toasts, Scots offered Scottish toasts, and Englishmen offered English toasts. At last, Scrooge himself interrupted them, thanked them for their many good wishes, urged them to continue to enjoy the hospitality for as long as they wished, and said it was time for him to whisk the bride away, as she had had a very long day and needed to find some peace and repose before she was totally exhausted. "Besides," he said, "she has confided to me that her shoes are killing her!"

So, amidst continuing cheers, handshakes, busses, embraces, and joyous good wishes, they made their way toward the exit, where Tiny Tim, Peter, and some other young men were standing by with their coats and hats and scarves, and then conducted them out to the curb, where Wilf was waiting with the beautiful carriage. "All right, Wilf," said Scrooge as he tucked a blanket around his wife's legs and leaned out of the carriage window, "let's go home!"

By prearrangement, Wilf drove a few blocks, cut down to the left, then left again, so that soon the horses were clipping along through the edge of Russell Square. Annabelle happened to look out in time to see the Great Russell Hotel flying past the window, and exclaimed, "What's happening, Ebbie? There's the hotel! We've been going in a circle!"

"Never mind," said Scrooge. "I'm sure Wilf knows what he's doing."

"But – but we're not going in the right direction," she protested.

"Patience, my dear," said Scrooge. "I'm sure we'll get there soon."

About that time, the carriage slowed and Wilf turned the team into the driveway of number 79 Russell Square, where he pulled on the reins and halted the barouche. Instantly, there were two young men, one at either side of the carriage, opening their doors.

"Peter!" said Annabelle. "And Tim! Whatever are you boys doing here?! We're supposed to be going home."

"Ah, my dear," said Scrooge, coming around the carriage to join her. "We are home." "What?" she said, bewildered. "What do you mean?"

He gestured toward the handsome doorway of the house, which was adorned not only by his old door knocker but by an immense white bow. "This is your wedding present, my dear," he said. "A new house. And this carriage? This too is a wedding gift, and Wilf will be our permanent driver. Come on inside and meet the rest of the staff!"

Annabelle was completely, utterly, totally flabbergasted. For a moment, she could not move at all, but stood, speechless, staring at the front of the beautiful house. Then she turned and looked back across the leafless square to the Great Russell Hotel diagonally on the other side.

"You mean – ?" she said, unable to believe her eyes.

Scrooge laughed, and so did the others.

"Yes, my dear," he said, "this is our new home. And the hotel over there is our neighbor, or one of them. I am proud to be able to give you a wedding present of this scope and beauty, something I could not have done all those years ago when we were young. It is, in a way, my small attempt to make up for the lost years. I want you to have the happiest life a woman can have, for I know I shall have the happiest life that any man could ever have."

Almost blindly, as if in a stupor, she let him lead her up the steps to the front door and into the house, where Wilf's family was waiting to greet them. Wilf's wife Gertrude, who was as tiny as he was immense, and their daughter Jennifer curtsied, as if acknowledging royalty. Scrooge explained that they were living in the carriage apartment behind the main house and that Gertrude was filling in as a cook until they could interview some people and choose one of her own liking. Jennifer, he said, would be helping around the house for the time being, and was available for service beyond that if things worked out for her to do so. They had a son, he said, whose name was Jason, and Jason was seeing to the horses.

"Your girl Ginnie will be here in a little while," he added, "to continue as your personal domestic. I expect she's having a final dance and maybe another glass of champagne before she leaves the hotel."

Gertrude had fixed a lovely, simple meal, knowing they would be too exhausted to eat a lot, and she and Jennifer served it by candlelight on the great table in the dining room. Scrooge had insisted that they sit and eat with them, and that Wilf and Jason be there too, so they could all get to know one another and enjoy the quiet together after such a busy weekend. Annabelle kept staring at Wilf, and Scrooge knew it was because of his great size, for he himself had been fascinated by Wilf when they first became acquainted.

At last, when the meal was over and the Tarkingtons, after cleaning up the dishes, had retreated to their own abode in the rear, Scrooge and Annabelle sat together before a blazing fire in the library, having a glass of brandy.

She shook her head as if she were in a perfect daze.

"I can't get over it, Ebbie," she said. "It's too much to take in!"

Chapter 12

Christmas Wedding

He smiled. He had hoped to produce an effect of wonderment in her, but had not expected it to be nearly so great. "You don't have to take it all in now, my love," he said. "It will require some getting used to. But I wanted our lives to be very different, now that we're married. I wanted you to enjoy a quality of existence beyond any you'd ever dreamed about, and I am looking forward to sharing it with you. The beautiful thing is that, while we shall be enjoying a wonderful life together, we'll also be blessing other people. Wilf and his family and Tim and Ginnie and whoever else we take on will be helped by being part of our larger family, and you and I will benefit from their joy and wellbeing."

She gazed at him in admiration. Little Ebbie Scrooge, the boy she had adored when they were in their teens. And now she was married to him. A man of great substance in the city, noted for his generosity and leadership. A man who dined with mayors and M.P.s and councilmen. A man whose name was known by thousands, her husband! She toyed with the word. Her husband! The man she would live with for the rest of her life. A man of enormous influence and inestimable gifts. A man who blessed others all around him, wherever he went, so that he seemed to preside over a veritable moving paradise. Her husband!

And as for Scrooge, he couldn't remember when he'd ever been happier. In fact, he couldn't remember when he'd ever even dreamed of such unparalleled happiness, such complete and unsullied joy. It was as if he were living in a dream and might wake up at any moment. But it was such a wonderful dream that he knew he would be pleased, even if he were to be awakened, by the residue of happiness it had deposited in his heart. His wife! The beautiful Annabelle, his precious Belle, after all those years of loneliness and deprivation, all that self-inflicted pain and burden brought about by his blind ambitions, now his, the sun and the moon and the stars, the empress of his affections, the love of his life. His wife!

In a few days time, life for Ebenezer and Annabelle began to settle into its new routine, and their comings and goings from 79 Russell Square soon became as natural to them as their lives before they were joined in marriage. They took "discovery" walks, as Scrooge liked to call them, in the neighborhoods around their own, strolling arm in arm and marking in their memories the particularly

gracious homes, the little businesses, and the convenience of a number of small parks or parklike spaces. They made numerous visits to the great British Museum, only two blocks away, where they lingered over the manuscripts of famous writers, the tombs of Egyptian pharaohs, and the visible reminders of Britain's far-flung empire, stretching to India in the East, Canada in the West, and the intriguing domains of Africa to the South. Sometimes they paused for refreshments in the museum's comfortable cafe. Other times they found delightful little restaurants of various cuisines – Indian, Chinese, Thai, German, Hungarian, and, of course, French and Italian – in the back streets of their area, and occasionally they even ventured back to the Great Russell Hotel, the site of their wedding reception, and had a more substantial meal there before returning to number 79 Russell Square. Annabelle got in the habit of having her friends in for lunch or tea, and, with the help of a delightful West Yorkshire woman named Mrs. Holyrood she had employed as her cook, her former maid Ginnie, and young Jennifer Tarkington, who continued as a part-time household assistant, made such occasions both frequent and stimulating, for, in addition to the excellent food, she often invited some person of note, an actor or singer or university scholar, to meet with them and perform a small program in exchange for a fine meal and the admiration of those assembled. Scrooge, for his part, worked almost as hard as ever, but found time to join a new club in the West End, one to which Captain Twiddle had introduced him, and frequently took his meal there if Annabelle was entertaining at home. He quickly became a favorite of the bellmen and waiters at the club, for he was the most lavish tipper any of them had ever known, and it was "Mr. Scrooge, sir" this and "Mr. Scrooge, sir" that on every hand. "Is that chair comfortable for you, Mr. Scrooge?" "Would you like a refill, Mr. Scrooge?" "What can I bring you, Mr. Scrooge?"

None of these lads, in Scrooge's estimate, were as fine and handsome as his own young valet, Tim Cratchit, who had fit in beautifully with the other staff members at number 79. Tim seemed to take an inordinate pride in seeing that Scrooge's clothes were carefully hung when he took them off, and brushed and laid out properly when he was preparing to go out. "You have put such a shine upon my shoes," exclaimed Scrooge one day, "that they are positively blinding, my boy!" The new cook, Mrs. Holyrood, was proving equally worthy as a chef. Annabelle had chosen her from a number of applicants she'd interviewed, as much for the pleasantness of her manner as for her undeniable culinary skills. She and Tim and Ginnie and Jennifer all got along like musketeers, laughing and chatting and being generally supportive of one another, so that they were a most agreeable part of the extended family. They worked so well together, in fact, that Scrooge and Annabelle agreed that for the time being they would not bother with employing a butler, lest the introduction of another servant in the household, and one with more authority than the others, should upset the delightful atmosphere that now obtained.

For the first time, under Annabelle's capable guidance, Scrooge experienced the delights of foreign travel, which he found exhilarating not only because of the childlike pleasure it afforded Annabelle but

for the many agreeable citizens he met wherever they went. Their very first trip was to Paris, for a "belated honeymoon" in the springtime, as Scrooge called it. They stayed at the Hotel Georges Cinq, strolled the Champs Elysee, visited the Louvre, had luncheons at little sidewalk cafes on the Left Bank, and at night had their dinner on one of the many bateaux mouches, the amiable floating restaurants on the River Seine. Another time they journeyed to Florence and Rome, savoring the wonders of layers upon layers of old cultures, from the Sistine Chapel at the Vatican to the flea market at the heart of Florence. Going on by train to Venice, they strolled through the vast Cathedral of St. Mark, took gondola rides on the beautiful canals, and visited the famous glass factory at Murano, where Scrooge bought Annabelle twenty-four very delicate cobalt-blue cups and saucers trimmed in gold and decorative porcelain, which she said would be the delight of her tea parties back home. In Switzerland they stayed in a lakeside cottage in Lucerne, where they learned to enjoy cheese fondue, visited the chalky blue waters of the stream at Interlocken, climbed partway up the Matterhorn, and were entertained by yodelers and accordionists whose lilting melodies made them want to dance until morning, although they usually had the good sense to be in bed by midnight.

"You have shown me the world!" exclaimed Annabelle one day as they were crossing the Channel back into England's fair and pleasant land. "My late husband Mr. Moore always talked of traveling too, but we never got farther than Edinburgh in the North and Exeter in the West Country. The poor man was always busy, the way you were when I first knew you, Ebbie dear."

Scrooge chuckled. "So you gave up one busy man for another," he remarked in a rare show of playfulness.

"Oh yes," she said. "But I got the first back as a different person, and I'm so happy I did!"

Their social life in London seemed to expand and expand, as if there were no limits to it. Even the Prince of Wales and his current mistress dined with them on occasion, and once their table was graced in the same evening by the young Mr. George Bernard Shaw, who was just becoming established as a major playwright in England, and the venerable Charles Dickens, whose home, they discovered, was only a few blocks away from their own. The exchange between the two gentlemen was electric. At one point, Mr. Shaw proposed that he turn Mr. Dickens' novel A Tale of Two Cities - the one beginning "It was the best of times, it was the worst of times" - into a stage play, but Dickens ridiculed the idea, asserting that two or three hours of action and speeches on a London stage could not begin to compete with a good novel for people's attention. In fact, he suggested, it would be much better if Mr. Shaw were to permit him to turn one of his plays, say, Arms and the Man, into a rollicking good novel, with dozens more characters and enough bracing description to transform the creation into a true work of art.

The Scrooges became such a fashionable part of London society that in their third year of marriage they were invited to dine with Her Majesty, the Queen, at Buckingham Palace. For the occasion, Annabelle visited one of London's most famous couturiers and was outfitted with a beautiful emerald-green gown, for which Scrooge went out and bought her an enormously expensive silver necklace with a huge emerald pendant. She told him she could never wear such a costly ornament, but

once she had tried it on he could not pry it away from her if he attempted to do so, which he didn't. He himself was somewhat spruced up for the occasion with a shiny red satin sash, which he wore across his chest from the left shoulder to the right side of his waist. He also wore a heavy gold medallion awarded him a few years earlier by the Lord Mayor of London for his charitable works in the city and his support for the Lord Mayor's policies. Even Wilf was outfitted with a newuniform for the palace visit, for he must never feel ashamed, Scrooge thought, before the grooms and drivers of other elegant carriages.

As Scrooge and Annabelle lay in bed that night, they talked about the evening and how they had experienced it. Annabelle said that she had no idea the Queen had become so portly, and Scrooge said that it fitted her dour nature, for he had not observed her to laugh a single time at anything that was said, even though there were some monstrous things vouchsafed by some of the guests, and had witnessed her almost smiling only once, when Viscount Steltingham stepped on a boiled egg he had inadvertently dropped beside his chair and, reaching out for something to save his fall, grabbed hold of his wife's gown and pulled her onto the floor on top of him. Two things of emotional significance to the newly married Scrooges occurred not long after their wedding.

First was the engagement and subsequent marriage of young Peter Cratchit and Margaret Hennessey, Annabelle's widowed daughter. Peter had developed so much confidence in Scrooge that he besought him several weeks in advance about the wisdom of proceeding to marriage so soon after his acquaintanceship with Mrs. Hennessey. Scrooge, pleased that the young man had sought his advice, said that he was perhaps not the best source of information about such things, as he had botched his own engagement plans when he was Peter's age, but that, in light of his experience stemming from that failure, he was all in favor of marrying as soon as a man established that the young woman of his choice was likely to be the love of his life forever. This was all the encouragement Peter needed, and so he intensified his courtship with Mrs. Hennessy and, shortly after Easter, while they strolled through the park on a Sunday afternoon, offered his proposal and placed a modest gold ring on her finger.

Like many couples, they favored a June wedding, and, as they had been greatly impressed by the Rev. Mr. Plumwood, who read the marriage service for Scrooge and Annabelle, they promptly sought out the old rector and got a date on his calendar to marry them near the end of that month.

Scrooge himself volunteered to pay for the service, saying it was the least he could do for the altar of love, and involved his own dear wife in the planning of everything, inasmuch as it was her daughter who was being wed. Annabelle took Margaret shopping for a trousseau and helped her with many details about both the wedding and the reception to follow, which it was decided, because it would not be a huge wedding such as she and Scrooge had enjoyed, would be staged in the church hall at St. Martin's. There were flowers to be ordered, the catering of the food to be arranged, and many other details, for which Margaret was profoundly grateful, both to her mother and to Scrooge.

Peter asked his father, Bob Cratchit, to serve as his best man, which Bob was only too happy to do, and Margaret asked her sister Celia Crane to be her maid of honor, which assignment Celia both expected and was happy to fulfill. Scrooge himself volunteered to pay for the service, saying it was the least he could do for the altar of love, and involved his own dear wife in the planning of everything, inasmuch as it was her daughter who was being wed. Annabelle took Margaret shopping for a trousseau and helped her with many details about both the wedding and the reception to follow, which it was decided, because it would not be a huge wedding such as she and Scrooge had enjoyed, would be staged in the church hall at St. Martin's. There were flowers to be ordered, the catering of the food to be arranged, and many other details, for which Margaret was profoundly grateful, both to her mother and to Scrooge.

Peter asked his father, Bob Cratchit, to serve as his best man, which Bob was only too happy to do, and Margaret asked her sister Celia Crane to be her maid of honor, which assignment Celia both expected and was happy to fulfill.

"Now," said Margaret at dinner one evening with Scrooge and Annabelle, "we have everything just about arranged. Peter has a best man and I have a maid of honor. We also have a minister. So I suppose the only thing lacking at this point is someone to walk me down the aisle. Father Ebenezer, I thought that might be something you'd be willing to do. Would you?"

Scrooge was of course delighted to be asked, and hastily agreed.

There was rain falling heavily on the church when they arrived for the wedding, so that all one might observe from a post across the street was a sea of large black umbrellas jostling about in the churchyard and up to the church doors. But thankfully, by the time they were halfway through the service, the sun reappeared, weakly at first and then shining bravely, so that Mrs.

Cratchit turned to her son Tim and said, "Oh, Tim, hit's an omen, 'rnt it? I mean, they says rain at a weddin' is a blessin', but some'ow I feels that the sun's comin' out that way is a super-blessin', so to speak, a blessin' on top of a blessin'. Don't ye agree?"

Tim patted her arm and said that he certainly did. Peter and Margaret were going to have a wonderful life together or his name wasn't Timothy Cratchit!

The second thing of emotional importance to the Scrooges and the intimate circle of friends around them was that even then Bob Cratchit was beginning to feel the gnawing pains in his stomach that would eventually, some six weeks later, send him to a doctor, Scrooge's own physician in Harley Street, the eminent surgeon Dr. Russell Armentrout, for a check-up.

"I'm sorry to tell you, Mr. Cratchit," said Dr. Armentrout after a thorough physical examination of his patient, "but I fear it is bad news."

Chapter 13

The New Home

"Bad news?" asked Bob, adjusting his tie and trying to look nonchalant.

"Yes. You have all the symptoms of stomach cancer."

"What— what can be done, doctor?" asked Bob.

The distinguished looking physician shook his head slightly and frowned.

"Very little, I'm afraid," he said. "I can give you some medicine that will ease the pain, advise you about the best diet. But beyond that, our science has not really progressed very much. There are a few surgeons who would take your money and operate on you, but the evidence is not supportive of such an action. In most cases, the patient is actually worse for having had his intestines invaded in that manner. You can consult another physician, of course, and might receive an entirely different opinion, but I doubt it. That's up to you."

Bob was nonplussed. He had not expected such a gloomy diagnosis, and had entered the doctor's surgery believing that he would emerge with a bottle of elixir and soon be feeling right as rain again. How would he tell his wife?

Eventually, he recovered the presence of mind to ask, "You mean, I'm going to die? How long will I have? Can you tell me that?"

"Hard to say," said the doctor. "These things differ widely. You're a fit man. You might have a year, maybe even two. Then again —" His voice trailed off fatalistically. Bob did not wish to tell Mrs. Cratchit right away. He needed some time to formulate the words that would inform her without inducing the sudden panic he imagined she would feel.

It was to Scrooge he turned before telling his wife. They were in Scrooge's office, and Scrooge could tell there was some bad news. He could see it on Bob's countenance.

"You saw Dr. Armentrout yesterday," began Scrooge. "Did he give you a bad report?"

Bob Cratchit lowered his head, then, without speaking a word, raised his eyes to meet Scrooge's.

"I'm sorry, Bob. What did he say?"

Bob poured out the whole story of his examination and the doctor's diagnosis, and ended by saying, "I haven't yet told the missus. Frankly, sir, I don't know exactly how to do it. I know it will be a shock to her, however I do it."

Scrooge shook his head in agreement. "It will, Bob. You're very right about that. It is a shock to me, and I know it will be much worse for her." Then, after a moment's thought, he asked, "Would you like me to do it for you?"

Bob considered the offer, then shook his head no. "I'll have to do it myself," he said. "Hard as it is, it will have to come from me."

"Has she asked about the doctor's report?"

"Yes, sir, but I sort of put her off. Fact is, I told her it was nothing, that he said I'd be all right after taking some medicine he gave me." "Ah. Now you've got to reverse the news."

Bob nodded.

"I'll tell you what," said Scrooge. "Why don't you let me talk to Belle about it tonight, if you don't mind her knowing, and I'll ask her what you should do. Women are often wiser about these things, especially when it's a woman who's involved in receiving the news."

Bob brightened at the idea and said he would be very grateful if Scrooge would do that.

Annabelle was as broken up as Scrooge about the news. "He's right, you know, Ebbie. It needs to come from him. If it were our case and not theirs, poor dears, I would want to hear it from you. But surely there's something we can do to make it a bit easier."

"I know," she said after a few moments' thought. "Let's invite the Cratchits for dinner the night after Bob breaks the news to his wife. That way they'll have something to be looking forward to, and, hard as it is, they will come and we can introduce the subject then and talk with them about it. That should make it a little easier, if anything can at a time like this."

Scrooge agreed, and that is precisely what they did.

By the time the Cratchits entered the house, with Bob somber and his wife obviously heavily smitten by grief, Mrs. Cratchit had had some time to digest the sad meaning of Bob's report. Now she needed help thinking about all the implications. They ate first, and Jennifer cleared the table. Then they sat over their coffee to talk.

Scrooge brought it up. "Mrs. Cratchit," he said, "we know about Bob's awful news. I pried it out of him when he came back to the office. I took the liberty of telling Belle, as I knew she would understand. Now we are here to offer ourselves for anything we can do to help, either now or in the future. We go back a long way together, and have weathered many a storm. I hope that entitles us to stand near you in this difficult time, to offer a shoulder to weep on or a hand to help with anything that needs doing."

Mrs. Cratchit was in tears. "I know," she sobbed, "an' ye're right, Mr. Scrooge. We've knowed each other a long time, an' we count you amongst our dearest friends. They i'nt nothin' I wouldn't do fer you, and I know they's nothin' you wouldn't do fer me. It's jest —" She sobbed. "It's jest, I don't know what to do!

We've never 'ad to face anythin' like this afore. Maybe a little, when we nearly lost poor Tim. But this is diff'rent. Bob's me right hand. 'E's the other side o' me. We're — you know, we're a unit, so t' speak, an' I don't know what I'll do wi'out 'im."

"Now, mother," said Bob kindly, laying a hand on her arm, "the doctor didn't exactly say how much longer I have. Could be a coupla years, he said. They don't know these things. But we can't spend the time I got left worryin' about how it's gonna be or what'l happen to you and the children."

Chapter 14

Married Life Begins

"You don't worry about that," interjected Scrooge. "Your children will be well taken care of. I assure you of that."

Bob looked gratefully at Scrooge. "I know, sir. You're right, sir. You've been mighty good to me and my family, and I know I can trust you to see they're looked after when I'm gone."

"All right, then," said Scrooge. "That much is settled, at least. There'll be no worry about what will happen to your good wife and those beautiful children. They are part of our family, Belle's and mine. Our main concern then is for you to remain strong as long as you can, and to be as comfortable as you can. I think the first thing you should do is plan a little holiday somewhere, either for the two of you or for you and the children. Go to the seashore for a week or two. Walk on the beach, sail in a boat, do things you've always wanted to do. Talk about what lies ahead, and make your promises to one another. Then, when you come back, you should take more time off to spend with your wife and family, say, an extra day a week. And, when you get to feeling too poorly to work, well, that'll be the time to say so and stop coming into the office."

Bob looked hopefully at his wife. "That'd be nice, wouldn't it, dear? Coupla weeks at the seashore with the kids. We've never done that. Would you like that? We could get us some beach outfits, and some nice sandals and all, and we could have us a real holiday." Mrs. Cratchit smiled at him and wiped away more tears. She nodded her head in silent affirmation. The next day, at the office, Scrooge went into Bob Cratchit's accounting room and said, "Bob, I got to thinking after you and your missus went home last night. Your boy Peter is coming along well, don't you think?"

"Oh, yes, sir, Mr. Scrooge. Peter's a whiz. I'm real proud of him."

"Then let me make a suggestion. Why not train him to take your place when you don't feel like doing this work any more? I'm sure he's partway there now. But you could concentrate on seeing that he learns everything he needs to know about our businesses, and how to manage all the things you manage. Of course, there'll never be another Bob Cratchit, and I'd swear to that. But your Peter will be the next best thing, and he could be ready to step right into your shoes, if that sounds good to you."

Bob Cratchit's eyes shone with appreciation. "It certainly does, Mr. Scrooge. I know he could do it. He's a smart boy. And, as you say, he already knows a lot of what he'd need to know. I could take it in hand to double my input, and I'm sure he could replace me at almost any time!"

"Then let's do it," said Scrooge.

"The missus'll be proud," said Bob. "And I know it'll take a weight off her mind." "That's what we want, isn't it?" said Scrooge. "Oh, yes, sir, it is," replied Bob. "It certainly

It was only a month after the discovery of Bob Cratchit's medical condition that Scrooge was startled at his club one day by the approach of a very distinguished looking elderly gentleman he knew as Lord Burton because he had seen him from time to time and been told his name by attendants. He did not know him personally. It was almost a shock to Scrooge, therefore, to realize that Lord Burton was tottering in his direction and that, as there was no one else around, he must be intending to speak to him.

"You're Scrooge," said the old man in an unsteady voice.

"Yes, sir," said Scrooge, standing from the chair where he had been sitting and bowing slightly at the waist as a gesture of recognition of the gentleman's peerage. He would normally have extended a hand to shake, but realized that one did not do that with a peer of the realm before the peer first offered his hand.

Lord Burton stood there a moment, weaving back and forth slightly, and Scrooge wondered if there was something wrong and he was about to collapse and needed help.

Lord Burton nodded his head and said, "Good."

"Sir?" said Scrooge, not understanding. Again Lord Burton nodded. "I said, 'Good.' I heard at the palace last night that you're to be given an O.B.E.. Good man! Glad to hear it!" And with those cryptic remarks, he turned, or listed in another direction, and started to walk away. Scrooge wanted to call him back and ask for further explanation, but knew that such an action would have been deemed improper. Instead, he sat back in the big leather chair where he had been sitting before, and pondered the message he had just received. Could it be true? He himself had heard nothing of it. Surely the word would not be put out in advance of notification. Or would it? He had to admit he knew nothing of these matters. So it would be best simply to put it out of his head. Perhaps the old gentleman was confused.

The next day, at precisely ten o'clock in the morning, there was a rap on Scrooge's office door. He called out for the knocker to enter. The door opened, and one of the office assistants was there with another gentleman behind him. The other gentleman wore a dark suit, white shirt, tie, black overcoat, and bowler hat. "Gentleman to see you, sir," said the assistant, and backed out of the door, permitting the visitor to enter and face Scrooge.

"Mr. Scrooge," said the man in the tone of a senior clerk, who had the bearing of one as well. "I have brought a message from Her Royal Majesty, Queen Victoria. She invites you to the palace on

Wednesday, 1 November, three o'clock in the afternoon, to receive investiture as a member of the Order of the British Empire." As he said this, he produced an envelope, in heavy vellum with a royal seal on it, and handed it to Scrooge. What did one say to a messenger bearing this kind of message? Thank you? What's this all about? Can you explain the meaning?

Scrooge's instincts led him to do the right thing. He merely accepted the envelope, nodded to the messenger, and said, "Thank you. I shall be there."

Although he had many things yet to do, Scrooge felt totally undone for accomplishing them, so walked down to Fred McDougall's office to see if he was in. He wasn't.

All right, he needed to tell someone. So he got his coat and hat, went out to the corner, hailed a cab, and went home to tell Annabelle.

She was ecstatic!

"Oh, Ebbie," she said, "that's wonderful! And you deserve it, you certainly do! Who has done more for this city and this country than you have? Oh, I can't believe it! You'll be Lord Ebenezer, imagine. Oh, isn't it wonderful?!"

"And you'll be Lady Annabelle," he said.

She looked startled, for she hadn't thought of that.

"I will, won't I?" she said wonderingly. "Lady Annabelle. My, my! Who would ever have guessed it? Certainly I wouldn't. Oh, Ebbie. This is such fun, isn't it?!"

Chapter 15

A Fulfilling Life

"Oh," he said, for he had just thought of something.

"What is it?" she said.

"We weren't coming home until 5 November - Guy Fawkes' Day — remember?" "Well, we'll just have to change our plans. That's all there is to it."

For a couple of months, they had had a very big trip in the planning. He and Peter needed to go to India to finalize some deals they had set up there and to explore the possibility of other alliances as well. In his usual spirit of generosity, Scrooge had suggested that they take their wives and make a grand tour of it. They would visit Egypt and the Holy Land, then sail through the recently opened Suez Canal and on to India, visiting Bombay and Calcutta on business and then taking their wives to Agra to view the famous Taj Mahal.

Together with their wives, they had gone to a travel agency and made the arrangements. They would sail from Southampton on 8 September, arrive in Cairo on 13 September, take a smaller ship up the Nile River to see the pyramids, go on to Israel on 21 September, allow three weeks for seeing the many sights there, then go on to Rangoon, do their business at the ports, travel inland to Agra, and return to London by 5 November.

Bob Cratchit appeared to be holding his own. The medication the doctor had provided seemed to ease his intestinal pains considerably. So they weren't worried about anything's happening to him while they were away.

Annabelle and her daughter Margaret were of course excited about the prospects of such a long journey, and had spent several days in careful shopping, acquiring the kinds of clothing they were told would be necessary in the various climates they would visit. And Scrooge and Peter had made elaborate plans for their meetings with the heads of several businesses in India. "You're right," said Scrooge. "That's all there is for it. Peter can handle the business in India, and maybe he and Margaret would welcome a chance to be off by themselves for a while. I'll visit our travel agent and arrange for us to complete the first half of the trip, to Egypt and the Holy Land, and then we'll sail home and let the children go on alone."

"It isn't every day a man gets to join the O.B.E.," said Annabelle.

Scrooge smiled, quite satisfied with the idea of a change of plans. "You're right," he said. "It isn't every day."

"Look!" cried Margaret. "There's the Rock of Gibraltar!"

They were all standing on the top deck of the S.S. Dundee as the ship purred past the famous landmark and entered the Mediterranean. It had rained the day they pulled out of Southampton, but their staterooms were so pleasant, the food at dinner that evening was so good, and their companions at table were so amiable that they barely noticed, and by the next day the clouds had broken and the sun appeared, seeming to hail their passage into the calmer waters of the Mediterranean with a benediction of warmth and beauty.

Egypt, they found, was magnificent. All the stories they had heard of the impressiveness of the pyramids and their treasure-laden tombs were true. Scrooge and Annabelle had spent so many hours in the Egyptian rooms of the British Museum that they were not as impressed by the treasures as Peter and Margaret, but standing at the base of one of the great pyramids and marveling at the engineering feat of the Egyptian slaves who constructed it fairly took their breath away.

"Imagine!" said Scrooge. "They are easily among the great wonders of the world!"

If they were impressed by the monuments of Egypt, they were humbled by the experience of visiting the sites of Israel and imagining what they might have been like more than eighteen hundred years earlier when Christ walked the roads from Jericho to Jerusalem or taught the crowds on the hill beside the waters of Galilee. A sense of deep reverence fell upon all the members of their tour group, some of whom were from North America, Germany, and Scandinavia, and, along with most of the group, the four of them were baptized again in a simple ceremony at the edge of the River Jordan. Scrooge even obtained a bottle of water from the river to carry home to the Rev. Mr. Josiah Plumwood, knowing he would be thrilled to have it.

Once, when Scrooge and Annabelle were dining with a couple from Cincinnati, Ohio, in the United States, Annabelle dropped into the conversation the fact that she and her husband were having to cancel plans to go on to India because he had to be back in England to receive an O.B.E. "O.B. what?" asked the American wife.

"O.B.E.," clarified Annabelle. "It stands for 'Order of the British Empire.'"

"But I thought you were English," said the woman. "We are," said Annabelle patiently. "This is a special recognition of my husband for his years of philanthropic work."

"Oh?" said the American husband. "What kind of work is that? You mean, you give away money?"

Scrooge blushed, and smiled an embarrassed smile. "Perhaps," he said. "But I work with a number of organizations in behalf of the poor and indigent of our country. You know, hospitals, poor houses, that sort of thing."

"Are you connected with the Salvation Army?" persisted the man, saying he had heard about General William Booth and his good works.

"No," said Scrooge, "but General Booth and his organization are doing a fine work among the poor."

Annabelle, a little miffed at the obtuseness of the Americans, said that when her husband received the honor from the Queen he would become Sir Ebenezer.

"Oh," said the American wife. "That's nice."

Scrooge laughed about it when he and Annabelle were alone again. "If you are going to put on the dog," he chided his wife, "then you must do it with people who have some experience of kennels."

Before leaving Jerusalem, the Scrooges made a point of visiting the little tourist shops to collect mementoes they thought would be treasured by friends back home – bits of wood from the hulks of old Galilean fishing boats ("Who knows, madam, this might have come from the very craft in which Jesus and his disciples sailed"), stones from the ancient temple whose destruction was predicted by Christ, glass pendants containing a mustard seed ("Like the one Jesus spoke about in his parable, you know"), small crosses made from old trees on the Mount of Olives, and vials of water from the Jordan River, the Sea of Galilee, and the Dead Sea. They also bought numerous postcards with photographs of such holy sites as the Mount of Transfiguration, the Valley of Gehenna, Jacob's Well, the village of Bethlehem, the Garden of Gethsemane, the hill of Crucifixion, and the tomb from which, some British archaeologist had determined, Jesus emerged.

They hugged and kissed young Peter and Margaret as they parted from them at the seaport, wishing them a pleasant and inspiring journey on to India, and then boarded an Italian liner, the Colombo, bound for Portsmouth and their train back to London.

When they arrived in London, Wilf Tarkington was at the station to meet them.

Chapter 16

Bob Cratchit's Illness

"You needn't have bothered, Wilf," said Scrooge. "We could have taken a cab." "Not after the long journey you and the missus 'ave been on, sir," said Wilf. "You needs a bit o' cossetin', you do. Nothin' like yer own carriage f'r that, sir."

"Right you are, Wilf," said Annabelle. "I won't speak for Mr. Scrooge, but I could use 'a bit of cossetin',' as you put it, for myself." Fred McDougall had sent word to the house that he and Nessa had made reservations at the Great Russell Hotel dining room for the four of them that evening, and would meet them there at seven o'clock.

Scrooge supposed it was to catch him up on any business or financial events that had occurred in their absence, but the McDougalls' solemn faces after their initial hugs and greetings told him otherwise.

"We didn't want to wire you and dampen your spirits on the trip," said Fred, "but poor Bob has taken worse. The doctors reckon now it's only a matter of weeks, perhaps even days."

"They're administering morphine," said Nessa, "which makes his pain more bearable. Poor man. Mrs. Cratchit says it will be a blessing when he goes, as much as she dreads the day."

Thus the joy of their reunion was instantly siphoned off by the awful news of Bob Cratchit's condition. Yet Fred and Nessa still pressed them for details of their journey, which they were glad to provide if only to escape the immediate contemplation of the impending loss of their dear friend and partner.

As soon as Scrooge had attended to some of the many reports that had piled up on his desk during his absence, he and Annabelle made their first of many visits to the Cratchits' house, where they attempted to cheer poor Bob and sat for a long spell with Mrs. Cratchit, listening to her woeful voice as she lamented their tearful situation. "I don't know what I'll do wi'out 'im, I don't." she said. "E's been the light o' me life fer nigh onto fifty years, 'e 'as, an' I can see nothin' but darkness wi'out him, bless 'is 'eart."

There was little either Ebenezer or Annabelle could say to ease her grief, though they both assured her that somehow she would manage to survive the loss, as others did, and that she need not concern herself about any financial worries, for Scrooge would see to everything.

"We'll all miss him, Mrs. Cratchit," said Scrooge. "Our loss can't compare with yours, of course, but Bob Cratchit has been my right hand and arm for many years now, and no day will be the same without him on this earth, I can tell you that."

He meant it, for his own soul was sorely grieved by the ailing and imminent demise of this dear friend.

On the Sunday afternoon after their visit to the Cratchits' home, he had Wilf drive him out to the cemetery and allow him to walk through it to Marley's mausoleum, where he sat for a long time communing with the spirit of his old friend Jacob.

"You know how I must feel, Jacob," he said. "You knew Bob when he was only a youngster, and now he lightened up our offices, even when I was a dour old curmudgeon of an employer. I've never known another spirit to match his for simple cheeriness and enthusiasm. We went to see him the other day, and it made my heart heavy to behold the poor creature lying there in bed, a mere skeleton of his former self, half in and half out of life, but plainly suffering and ready to be gone."

Scrooge sat quietly for a few minutes, staring at Marley's statue. Once, a small bird lit on a shoulder of it, and Scrooge watched vacantly as it swooped away, having spotted something on the ground it wished to investigate more closely.

"This O.B.E. thing, Jacob – the knighthood – doesn't mean a thing to me now. Oh, I'm pleased for Belle. She seems to enjoy it, and will get some fun out of being called Lady Annabelle. But when I think of dear Bob lying there on his deathbed, I realize what an empty thing it is, a trifle, a mere charade, to be knighted by the Queen. What difference will it make? What possible difference? The initials after my name, I suppose. But what else? None at all, that I can think. It's merely part of the pageantry of life, the color and the dash, a little seasoning on the main dish, which is existence itself. I'd give it up in a moment to have Bob back in the office the way he was.

"You understand, don't you, Jacob? The way you understand everything now. How I wish we knew on this side of death all we're taught by even drawing near it! What changes we would work from our youth onward! How differently we would view things, what different goals we would pursue, how much it would transform our way of being, even the little things we say to one another in the passage of the day!" It was in that pensive mood that he returned to Annabelle that evening, so that she spoke to him, as they addressed the fire, "I know what's bothering you, my dear. It's Bob, isn't it? It affects me too, though I barely know him, compared to you. And Mrs. Cratchit, that poor, dear, simple soul. What she's going through right now! And Tim. Poor boy, he's so troubled by his father's problem. I don't know what God must be thinking."

Nor did Scrooge imagine what God might be thinking, and it troubled him. His faith had seemed so strong and vital only a few months ago, certainly when he and Annabelle were married and the throngs of well-wishers gathered around them. Now it seemed an insubstantial stick to lean upon, one no cripple would have chosen, and he felt that he was indeed a cripple.

He went through the ceremony of investiture on the first of November as solemnly as a judge, or as the occasion called for, and heard the Queen murmur a few words as she touched the royal sword upon his shoulders. But what did it all mean, he wondered. What did anything mean in such a world as this? It was a resplendent occasion, and Annabelle was enthralled by it, as were Celia and Delbert Newsome Crane and Fred and Nessa McDougall, who accompanied them – all the high and mighty folk, the dignitaries of state and church, the costumed finery, the sheer number of swords clinking at men's sides, the snapping of heels, the pomp and circumstance, the awarding of the garter with the words Onni soit qui mal y pense upon it – "Evil to him who thinks evil." Yet Scrooge was immeasurably saddened by it all, for he kept seeing poor Bob upon his deathbed, and his soon-to-be widow weeping at his side. And he thought of Bob and Tim, and their wonderful relationship. What mattered pomp and circumstance in the face of such terrible desolation, the dark maw at the end of life, hungrily devouring all whose existence faltered and collapsed upon its threshold?

Annabelle saw the cloud on his countenance, and it dampened her own enthusiasm as well, but she knew there was nothing she could say or do that might dispel it before its time. She could only observe, and wait, and pray. Thus it is with any of us whose mate has fallen under such a dark and hopeless spell. She smiled, but only on the surface, for down below, her heart was aching. She knew, she sensed, she felt it as if it were her own, the awful pain that was gripping her dear husband's soul and would not let it go.

The Order of the British Empire did no harm to Scrooge's far-flung business interests, to be sure. The English always loved titles of various kinds, even the more fictitious ones, and they had inordinate respect for anyone whose name was shadowed by the initials O.B.E., for they knew how small and select a company that placed him in. Scrooge the canny businessman. Scrooge the great philanthropist.

Scrooge the faithful churchman. Scrooge the tireless benefactor. Scrooge the perennial committeeman. Scrooge the center of power and influence. His name on any project was enough to guarantee its funding and success. His nomination was enough to secure any man's employment or promotion. Even his initials, E.S., were enough to tip the scales in favor of legislation. So his business interests throve, and more and more ships plied the seas to transport the goods his companies sold or the raw materials required to furnish them.

There were articles about him regularly in the newspapers and journals, and photographers were eager to capture pictures of him attending a meeting, dining with other businessmen, entering or leaving his club, or doing almost anything at all. It didn't matter, they simply wanted his photograph, for people were eager to see him and hear of his exploits.

In spite of Scrooge's feeling somehow ill used by Dickens's story about him, he and Dickens soon fell into a kind of natural camaraderie, for both loved the city and cared inordinately about the poor who inhabited its least fortunate areas. Attracted to Scrooge's propensity for helping people in need, Dickens soon took to exploiting that generosity; and was conveying the benefactor on his own special tours of waterfront communities along the Thames and other boroughs where life was cheap and crowds of people lived in squalid tenements thatreeked of crime, starvation, and human depravity. More than once the two men had been set upon by thugs and variets in this teeming underworld, so that a special bond was established between them by the very fact that they were fellow survivors. Both men were sympathetic to the denizens of these boundary areas and, even if they did not always carry large amounts of cash on them for fear of being murdered for their wallets alone, they made certain at least to provide the people for whom they felt pity the address of Scrooge's office, so that there was an almost constant stream of suppliants there, men, women, and children whose appearance was that of beggars and whose unwashed bodies guaranteed an aura of foulness that only Scrooge himself seemed capable of enduring. "Scrooge," Dickens once remarked, "you are the only man in London with a soul to match the needs of this forlorn humanity which, ironically, has been produced by the greatest economic engine in history. I say, 'Thank God for you, sir!'"

The brotherhood that grew between them through their frequent sojourns into the nether world of broken, all but irredeemable humanity made it doubly hard on Scrooge when his estimable companion began to show signs of terminal deterioration. First it was the vascular degeneration in one leg, which made it extremely painful for him to stand or walk, and which was rendered all the more intolerable by the inhuman schedule of the author's reading engagements. Many of these engagements lay in Scotland and Ireland -- not to mention his great trips to America -- and called for extensive rail travel, which Dickens found not only uncomfortable but unbearably frightening. Often, when Dickens arrived at his destination, he would feel too ill to go on stage. Yet go on he did, for he held a great reverence for his own audiences and would not abstain from performing even if he must do so at an incredible price to himself.

Dickens and Mrs. Dickens had not gotten along well for years, and he often confided to Scrooge that one of the delights of being in the Scrooge household was the opportunity to behold a married couple still obviously enthralled by one another. He had a fine home at Gad's Hill Place, a distance from London, but because of his frequent business in the city he acquired another home at 5 Hyde Park Court, where he often repaired for weeks at a time. It was there that Scrooge usually descended upon him, bearing flowers, books, and candy as remembrances of their friendship and assurances of the latter's continuing good will.

When Dickens was able, they often met in a favorite coffee shop, Commander's in Soho, and sat for hours discussing their philosophies of life and the adventures they had experienced. Scrooge had no children of his own, but Dickens possessed ten, and Scrooge was fond of drawing him out about this or that one. Two sons had gone to Australia to make their own way in the world, and a letter from either of them was always a subject of interest to the two gentlemen as they sipped their favorite brew.

Once, Scrooge had brought young Tim Cratchit with him to the coffee shop, for he wanted him to meet the famous author who had immortalized him in a story. Dickens, obviously touched by Tim's modesty and comeliness as a person, spoke very kindly to him, and Tim, in turn, stood plainly in awe of

Chapter 17

The O.B.E.

the novelist who in his time stood head and shoulders above all the rest. On the next occasion when Dickens and Scrooge were together, Dickens brought along an inscribed copy of A Christmas Carol for Scrooge to carry to Tim, and Tim clearly valued it above every other treasure he possessed. When Dickens eventually passed on after several weeks of confinement at his Gad's Hill home, Scrooge was strangely and deeply affected by the death, and seemed to mourn the loss of his friend more than anyone else in all of London, even though the famous writer's passing was a source of near cataclysmic grief in the entire nation. For days, he wore his black armband and stood across the street from the house in Hyde Park Court where he had so often visited his friend, too numb of soul to pay attention to whether the sun was shining or there was snow and ice upon the ground.

"Why?" he asked his friend Marley when he visited his tomb. "Why are things the way they are, Jacob? Why do bad men -- men without care or scruples or destination -- walk the streets, while a man like Charles Dickens, filled with grace and understanding as few men are, is struck down and carried off? Can God possibly be found righteous in the death of such a man?"

He had asked a similar question of his friend, the Rev. Mr. Josiah Plumwood, on more than one occasion, and Mr. Plumwood would produce some vague, circuitous argument from the depths of his theological bowels, mainly about the unquestionableness of divine ways and the indefensible sordidness of the human soul. These answers were always unsatisfactory to Scrooge, who had never felt any real agreement with Mr. Plumwood's theological disposition, but he seldom attempted to argue, finding their premises irreconcilable from the very start. Now, in Marley's presence, he complained of his rector's unflinching fidelity to the dourest views of old John Calvin, views to which he himself could offer no subscription whatsoever.

"It is more than I can understand, Jacob," he continued in his one-sided conversation, "how one could ever justify the deity's reckless and irresponsible choices of who should live and who should not. I raised the matter at dinner one evening with Browning -- you know the fellow, I'm sure -- Robert Browning -- has spent a lot of time in Italy -- and he said very little at the time. A few days later, however, he sent me a long poem he had written, one with a very peculiar title. I think it was 'Caliban upon Setebos.' Caliban was an ignorant native whose musings about his god Setebos gave voice to some of what I had expressed to Browning. He had this fellow Caliban throwing rocks to kill crabs as they passed beneath him at the water's edge. He allowed twenty crabs to pass without incident, then stoned the twenty-first, just like that. No rhyme, no reason. Just wham, bam, and started counting again. I wasn't sure, when I had read the thing, if he was making fun of my critique or not.

"Whether God is right or not, I cannot tell. The thing is, Jacob, I fear I may be losing my mind. I can't think straight. I waken in the night and can't get back to sleep for all the demons chattering on my bedpost. Everywhere I look, there's suffering and unhappiness. My own disposition, once so sunny and pleasurable, has sunk into a morass of darkness and dyspepsia. I know poor Belle is ready to chuck me out, or else to throw a blanket over me, stick me in a corner, and pretend I don't live there any more. I

don't know what to do, old friend. I'm losing my hold on life. My happiness has gone, evaporated. I can't even stand myself." Peter and Margaret Cratchit, meanwhile, were deeply saddened by the word when they reached home of Bob Cratchit's downward turn, and lost no time in rushing to his side to learn the worst. "If only we had known," mourned Margaret, "we could have come back with Mr. Scrooge and Annabelle. As wonderful as India was, and as much as Peter accomplished in the way of business, we wouldn't have thought a moment before turning home!"

Scrooge ordered Peter to spend as much time as possible with his father now that the end was approaching. "You can delegate your responsibilities at the office," he said. "Being with your father is the most important thing right now." He said almost the same thing to young Tim. "I can fend for myself, Tim, pleasant as it has been to have you for my valet. Right now, you must be at your father's side, and your mother's as well, for they will need you in this dark hour. You were always one to make them see the cheerful side of things, if there was one to see."

In all the gloom that pervaded the Cratchit and Scrooge households during this time, Peter and Margaret made a discovery that they hoped might release a modicum of joy: Margaret was pregnant. Annabelle was the first they told, and she behaved like any mother about to be made a grandmother for the first time, squealing and seizing her daughter in a tight embrace, then kissing the father and dancing around the room with him, already crafting plans for the little tot's arrival. Scrooge smiled when he was told, but didn't show sufficient enthusiasm for Annabelle's taste, and she chided him for it. "Well, it seems to me," she said scoldingly, "that you could be a little happier for them and stop moping around for at least ten minutes!"

The reception of the news was also mixed in the Cratchit household, where Bob tried to be pleasantly responsive for them but was obviously troubled by the realization that he would probably not be alive to greet the little one, and Mrs. Cratchit, entertaining the same realization, likewise attempted to be delighted but failed to be convincing to her son and daughter-in-law. "It's wonderful," she told them, "but I do so wish as Bob'd be 'ere to see it, our first gran'chile. Some 'ow hit don't seem right as 'e should 'ave to miss that."

The introduction of this expectation of a new child nevertheless worked a kind of spell over the entire family, for they talked of little else for the next few months. Annabelle helped Margaret plan the layette for the baby, and sought to ease her fears about the normal things young mothers-to-be-for-the-first-time often worry about. And it was a relief to see that Mrs. Cratchit was gradually transferring some of her deep affection from her husband Bob, who daily worsened, onto her hopes for this new child, who, male or female, was bound to be the prettiest, smartest, and best baby in the whole city of London. Even though she would not leave Bob's side long enough to help Margaret shop for things to prepare for the birth, she was kept abreast of every purchase, every thought, and every impulse, and, when the expectant mother felt the baby's kicking, was the first to be informed and invited to lay her hand upon the mother's stomach. All in all, it seemed a blessing for the baby to be coming at such a time, when its Grandfather Cratchit had such a precarious hold upon life itself.

Then misfortune struck. Little Nell, Fred and Nessa's daughter, fell ill with a high fever, and, within an hour or two, had broken out with a dreadful rash. Dr. Armentrout, summoned to their home, examined the child and pronounced that she had German measles. It was going around London at the moment, and he had seen at least a dozen cases among his own patients. "You must take precautions," he told the anxious parents, "for if you have not already had the measles yourselves, you are very likely to come down with them now."

Fortunately, the maid who worked for Nessa had had measles in her youth, and volunteered to move into the household to care for little Nell on an around-the-clock basis until the crisis was over.

But hardly had Nell begun to recover, so that her fever declined and she felt like eating again, when her mother broke into a rash herself. The illness was much harder on her as an adult than it had been on little Nell, and now the maid had two patients, not one, for whom to care. And two days later Margaret Cratchit erupted with the same kind of welts, so that there was no avoiding the fact that she had succumbed to the epidemic going around. Her case seemed lighter than poor Nessa's – in fact, her fever was not nearly so high and she appeared to be less listless – but the worry, of course, was for the baby she was carrying in her womb. German measles were almost always damaging, if not fatal, to unborn fetuses. "There isn't anything we can do," said Dr. Armentrout, "but wait and see if your child is affected. You can pray that it isn't, but there is no medication that has been proven effective against measles in the unborn."

Both mothers had recovered from the disease when Bob Cratchit died one evening shortly after dinner. His going was peaceful and undramatic, and, as it had been so long expected, was considered a blessing from heaven. He simply stopped breathing. His son Tim was in the room and leapt immediately to the elder Cratchit's side to be sure he had no pulse. Then quietly, without raising his voice, he walked into the kitchen where his mother was drying the supper dishes and Peter was studying a report and announced that their loved one, his and Peter's dear father and Mrs. Cratchit's husband, had departed from this life. Mrs. Cratchit emitted a slight gasp of surprise and they all hurried into the room where the corpse lay, his eyes still half open and his body in the desultory position where it had lain for the past few weeks.

The two boys stood reverently beside the bed as their mother collapsed upon their father in a small orgy of grief, and, when she had had her cry and removed herself from the bed, Peter closed his father's eyelids and pulled the coverlet over his face.

Tim himself came around to the Scrooges' house to inform them of his father's passing. Annabelle seized and held him desperately, hoping that this motherly act would suffice to express her own and Scrooge's intimate and heartfelt condolences. Scrooge himself merely turned away, appearing to stare out of the window onto Russell Square, and stood there in mute contemplation, or lack thereof, for fully a minute before saying, "I'm sorry, Tim. I truly am. Your father was like a son to me, and I am deeply moved by his going. I cannot tell you how desolate his passing leaves me."

A funeral service was held in the Cratchits' own church two days later, when a light snow had fallen upon the ground. Scrooge noticed as they bore the coffin into the burial ground the pairs of tracks made by the grave diggers as they had trodden to a distant section of the ground where there was still room for interments. "All tracks," he thought to himself, "lead eventually to the grave."

There was general weeping in the crowd as the casket was lowered into the grave and the clergyman, a Rev. Mr. Roof, uttered the words from the Prayerbook, "earth to earth, ashes to ashes, dust to dust," as he dribbled a sprinkling of dirt upon the wooden container. Scrooge barely heard these words, as he was still focusing upon the earlier words the minister had just spoken: "Man that is born of a woman hath but a short time to live, and is full of misery. He cometh up and is cut down, like a flower; he fleeth as it were a shadow... In the midst of life we are in death."

The words seemed to echo in his brain: "in death... in death... in death..."

Everything reeked of death. Annabelle had invited all the Cratchits back to 79 Russell Square for a repast after the service, and all but Peter and Margaret came. They excused themselves, saying that Margaret was tired and needed to rest.

"There was never a man like 'im," remarked Mrs. Cratchit over a cup of tea and some bread and butter, that being all she thought she could digest at the time. "'E were such fun, 'e were! Ever since we married, 'E were gentle an' lovin', not just t' me but t' ever'one, 'specially our younguns. If ever a better man did live, I knows not 'is name. Don't you agree, Mr. Scrooge?"

Scrooge said he must agree, Bob Cratchit was one in a million.

"Hit's Tim as'll miss 'im most, I reckon," she continued. "They become real close in Tim's early years, when 'e was so bad crippled and 'is dad 'ad to carry 'im most places we went. Ye remember that, Mr. Scrooge?"

Scrooge said that he did.

"There was a bond betwixt 'em unlike any other I've ever seed. One seemed t' know what t'other was thinkin'. They was more like mother 'n' daughter than father 'n' son, bein' so close an' all. Tim may not say much, but 'e'll be a-grievin', I can promise ye that. God he'p 'im, 'e'll be a-grievin' his pore 'eart out!"

Scrooge, unable to bear many more sad ruminations, excused himself and, seeking Wilf in the courtyard behind the house, asked him to drive him once more to the cemetery where Marley's tomb stood. There he walked through the dusting of snow, leaving the only prints in the entire place that day, and, ignoring the layer of snow, sat on his usual bench and stared into empty space for a few minutes. Eventually he spoke without adjusting his sight to look at Marley's statue: "I don't know how much more I can stand. Jacob. First, Dickens. Now, Bob. Bob was as dear a man to me as I have ever known, including your own dear self. He was such a sweet fellow. Never complained, even in the old days, when he hadn't tuppence to his name. He'd do anything I asked him to do, and do it cheerfully. He was such a good influence on all of us. And now he's gone."

Chapter 18

Travels and Society

He sat awhile in meditation before he spoke again. "'In the midst of life we are in death.' It's true, isn't it, Jacob? You know about such things. Death is everywhere. Even at our parties. Even when we're singing and dancing and having a good time. Even in church, death is there, staring at us, waiting to clasp us in its cold, clammy arms."

After another pause, he continued: "What's it all worth, Jacob? Why do we bother? Why aren't we simply snuffed out when we are born, saving everybody the trouble of growing up, struggling to make a living, having children, trying to make sense of things? That would be sensible, wouldn't it? Just bang us in the head when we're born and be done with it!"

He got up and walked around the monument, staring aimlessly at its lines and joints. He stood still a minute, then sat down again where he had sat before.

"Bob's death is bad enough in itself. But the really bad thing – what's on all our minds but nobody talks about – is what may happen when Margaret comes to term and that child of hers is born. It's almost certain to be disfigured, you know. Or have no mind to speak of. What will that do to young Peter and his wife? How will they cope without Bob to cheer them? He could've done, you know. He had a talent for it. He could make things seem better when they weren't, just by saying certain words."

He shook his head and watched the snow drift off his hat.

"I don't know, old partner," he said. "I just don't know."

Then, a few moments later, he said, "I don't know if I can make it any more. Everything's too sad!"

And, with those parting words, he rose and slowly walked back to the street, where Wilf and the carriage were waiting.

Scrooge's depression was beginning to take a toll on his relations with Annabelle. She could understand that things were bothering him, and sympathized. But she felt witless to combat this ponderously heavy mood. Sometimes, if she had the energy, she tried to humor him, to make him smile, to lift his dark spirits. But the efforts were almost always wasted. Occasionally he would look at her with a hint of the old gleam in his eyes, but only occasionally. Usually he simply went on staring into space, as if whatever she said or did had not registered at all. From time to time, he snapped at her. Afterwards, he was always ashamed, and apologized. But she felt the sting of his tongue, the tartness of his spirit, and it offended her. After all, she had done nothing to provoke this negative attitude. She herself was always cheerful and even-tempered. She comported herself as a lady, both in public and at home, and tried to maintain a sense of quiet dignity in their household. If he said anything hasty or unkind to the servants, she made a point of apologizing to them afterward, and saying that Mr. Scrooge was not himself, so they must forgive him.

Once he even spoke harshly to Tim. Tim had brought him his mail and laid it on the library table, where Scrooge was seated. Scrooge barked, "Why are you disturbing me now, boy? Can't you see I'm busy?" His regret surged almost instantly, and he managed to stammer, as Tim was leaving by the door, "I'm sorry, son. I don't know why I spoke like that. I hope you'll forgive me. I've not been feeling my best of late. Your father, you know."

A few days before Christmas, Margaret lost her baby. There was no warning. She and Peter were sitting at the breakfast table, as they usually did, having their toast and tea, when she suddenly experienced a horrible contraction that took her breath away.

"Oh!" she cried, and "Oh!" again.

Startled, Peter leapt up and asked, "What's wrong?"

"The baby!" she said. "I think it's coming!"

"I'll send for the doctor," said her husband.

Feeling an enormous pain that gripped her entire lower body, she gasped, "There isn't time! It's coming, Peter, it's coming! Help me into the other room. Let me lie on the sofa! And bring some towels! Quick, hurry!"

But she collapsed on the kitchen floor, and the poor little fetus, a boy, forced its way into the light, dying in the very act of making its appearance.

The doctor said it was the measles. They had infected her baby, and he would not have been normal even if she had carried him to term.

Peter was heart-broken, as Margaret was, and as were the baby's two grandmothers.

It was hard to tell how Scrooge took it, for he appeared stolid and unmoved. When the funeral for the little boy was held, he refused to go, saying he had had enough of death and dying.

Annabelle was angry with him.

"For once," she said, "you should think of someone other than yourself! Of course you don't want to go. Neither do I. But Margaret and Peter are grieving. They lost their baby. It would be heartless not to be there to support them. If you don't go, I – I –"

She could not finish her sentence, she was so exasperated.

Scrooge did not attend the funeral. At the hour when the others were at the church and cemetery, he went to his club.

"Sir Ebenezer," the bellman greeted him at the door. "We haven't seen you lately. What can I do for you, sir?" "Not a damn thing," said Scrooge in a low voice. "Just let me be!"

Removing his hat and coat, he handed them to the woman in the cloak room and climbed the wide marble steps to the second floor, where the lounge was empty and a roaring fire burned on one side of the room. Sinking into one of the heavy leather chairs beneath the cracked paint of old portraits, he put his head in his hands and kept it there for several minutes, feeling as if he had come to the end of the road and then, breaking through some invisible barrier, were in free fall, hurtling headlong into a dark abyss.

"Eeee-yah-h-h!" he suddenly shouted at the top of his voice, as if he were dispelling some terrible demon clutching at his throat.

Chapter 19

Charles Dickens

Several people on the floor, both patrons and waiters, came rushing in, supposing some poor chap had suffered a heart attack and died. What they saw was Scrooge sitting forward on the edge of his chair, his elbows on his knees and staring at them calmly, as if his exorcism had for the moment been successful.

"Is something wrong, sir?" asked one of the attendants.

"Sir Ebenezer," said one of the members, puzzled, "was it you who cried out like that?"

Scrooge merely looked at them and forced a little smile.

"Sorry," he said. "I couldn't help it."

And indeed he couldn't. When Scrooge returned home a few hours later, he found Annabelle packing a large suitcase.

"What's happening?" he asked. "Where are you going?"

For a moment she ignored him and continued packing.

At last she said, very soberly, "I told you yesterday. We're going to stay with Margaret and Peter for a while. My daughter needs me."

"Oh," he said. He didn't doubt that she had told him. He probably wasn't listening.

"You'd better pack as well," she said.

Scrooge stared at the suitcase on her bed, but seemed unable to move or speak. At last, he shook his head. "You go," he said. "I can't. I – I – can't."

She regarded him a moment and felt instantly sorry for him. But there was no denying her daughter's need right now. She was her mother, and therefore irreplaceable at such a time.

"All right," she said. "I'll speak to cook. She'll see that you have everything you need. Tim will be here, of course, and Jennifer. I will take Ginnie with me. I intended to ask Wilf to drive us over to Margaret's house, but now I think I'll ask Tommy Twiddle instead. He's already asked if there's anything he can do. He won't mind, and I won't interrupt things here by taking Wilf's time."

The horrible reality dawned on him. It was almost Christmas! How could she leave him so near the most special day of the year?! Their anniversary! And go with Tommy Twiddle! Had she been seeing Twiddle without his knowledge? What was going on? Was it something he should have known about?

He felt a peculiar sense of betrayal he had never known, and also a slight stab of panic. Belle was going without him — and with Twiddle. He had not been separated from her since their marriage. She was an indispensable part of his being. How would he continue without her? He knew he deserved her leaving, even with Twiddle. He had behaved like a complete ass. Margaret did need her. He could not blame her for going, if only to get away from him.

Even at Christmastime.

Was this the beginning of the end of their marriage? Again, he couldn't blame her if it was. She was such a good, sweet woman, so tolerant and long-suffering, and he had been behaving terribly. He knew it, but couldn't help it. Life for her would be much better without him. He could moan and groan all on his own, and her dear spirit would not be weighed down by his.

He felt an impulse to apologize, to say he would go, to beg her to stay, to remind her that it was nearly Christmas and she mustn't leave him now. But his feeling of total inertia would not permit him to go, and his sense of pride would not permit him to beg her to stay. If she needed to go, she must go, and that was all there was to it. Perhaps, in a few days, he would feel stronger, would be able to communicate to her that he had found his old self again and wanted her to come home. Somehow, it was a situation of his own making, unhappy as it was. There was nothing he could do but live with it.

Then he remembered the Christmas party.

"But you can't go!" he importuned. "The party! Wednesday is Christmas eve. We've never missed a company party. Everyone will expect us. You can't go now, Belle. At least wait until Christmas day, so we can make an appearance at the party!"

She looked at him with the kind of look wives often reserve for looking at their husbands. Slowly, she shook her head. "You don't understand, do you? This is my daughter we're talking about. Margaret needs me. She needs us. But if you won't go, I'm going without you. They can have the party without us, Ebenezer. Sometimes necessities override tradition. Besides, in the mood you're in, you won't make much of an impression at the party this year. You look a lot more like a wake than a party!"

Stung by her remark, Scrooge fell silent. She was right, he knew. He really didn't feel like attending the party. He would have to, he supposed, at least for a little while. But it would be an effort, especially without Belle at his side. Overcome by a sense of immeasurable sadness, he watched her close her suitcase. He followed her to the great foyer of the house, stood helplessly by as Ginnie carried her mistress's case and then her own to the front stoop, and looked on sadly while she assisted Belle in donning her fur-trimmed cape and matching hat. Belle, her appearance as elegant as ever, paused for a moment before exiting, then stepped over to her grieving husband and imparted a brief kiss to his cheek. Scrooge thought his world had crumbled as he beheld the two women climbing into Captain Twiddle's carriage, with Twiddle, as erect and effervescent as ever, attending them and making sure their laps were well covered by the handsome, fleecy blanket he produced. Scrooge stood mutely and absent-mindedly looking after them as the horses, their shoes echoing sharply on the frozen paving stones, bore them swiftly away.

That night, he rattled around in the house, unable to find contentment at anything or in any room. He tried to read, but the words failed to register. He watched the fire, but felt so lonely without Annabelle that the flames were like dancing devils, twisting and writhing in order to torment him. He tried to remember happy times, but whenever he did the present came crashing in upon him like a heavy weight and drove all the memories away. He even attempted to pray, confessing to God what a terrible creature he was. The Rev. Mr. Plumwood was right, he thought, man is a creature of depravity, for whom there is no hope apart from the sheer grace of the divine.

In the end, he dressed for bed and put on his nightcap, and, throwing more coal on the fire in his room, climbed into the great four-poster to listen to its crackling and watch the shadows dancing on the walls.

He was a portrait of pure, agitated misery!

Two days later, on Christmas eve, he was feeling more wretched than ever. He had not heard anything from Annabelle. The few servants were tiptoeing around him and being very guarded in whatever they said. He knew they had been discussing him, and he couldn't blame them, for he knew he was behaving like a horrible old curmudgeon. Nothing satisfied him. His porridge was too

Chapter 20

The Worm in Paradise

hot or too cold, his room too stuffy or too airy, his shirts too starched or too limp, the house too quiet or too noisy. Even young Tim, his valet, stayed out of his way most of the time, not wishing to incur his wrath.

At noon, he assembled the staff and told them to take the rest of the day off, and the night and the morrow, for that matter, as, with the exception of Wilf, who would be required to drive him to the Christmas party, he had no need of any of them and did not wish to hear them gossiping or sniggering about him. Jennifer and Jason, of course, lived with their folks in the mews behind the big house, but the Mrs. Holyrood, the cook, was happy to be able to visit her son and his wife in Canterbury and have Christmas with them, and Tim said that at the end of the party that evening he would go home with his mother, who would need the support, having recently lost not only her husband but her first grandchild. A little later, Scrooge stomped off to his club, where he behaved abominably to the staff. Whenever one of them wished him a merry Christmas, he found himself thinking, "Bah, humbug!" The very recurrence of the words, if only in his mind, unnerved him, for they symbolized a retrogression he dared not contemplate. He could tell the attendants were all looking for a generous tip, now that Christmas was upon them, but he scowled at them and thought, "Why should I pay you for service I don't want in the first place? What do you think Christmas is, anyway, an excuse for picking a man's pocket when you spread his napkin or bring him a bowl of soup?" It was the same as he walked along the street. Little groups of carolers stood in front of the stores, singing their hearts out about the birth of the Christ child, and somehow he felt outraged by their very presence. "Out of my way!" he commanded more than once. "Public nuisance!" he muttered as he walked around one group of carolers who were partially blocking the sidewalk.

He saw the crowds of people carrying presents, rushing about in their final preparations for Christmas, and their very busyness, even their apparent happiness, disgusted him. What was it all about, anyway? A Child born hundreds of years ago in some foreign country. A lot of tomfoolery created around an ill-founded, trumped-up holiday in order to sell things to people who didn't need them and couldn't afford them. "Bah, humbug!" he repeated several times as he wended his way back to 79 Russell Square. He would be glad when Christmas was over and people returned to their senses.

The house seemed unusually empty when he got back, for Mrs. Holyrood and Tim had left, and Jennifer and Jason were obviously staying with their family in the carriage house. Jason had laid kindling for fires in all the rooms, and there was a bucket of coal standing by each hearth. It was probably Tim who had left the note on the big dining room table that said, "Merry Christmas,

Mr. Scrooge." He crumpled it up and threw it into the fireplace, muttering "Bah! Humbug!" out loud as he did.

Merry Christmas, indeed! He couldn't remember when he had felt so miserable.

As much as he dreaded his company's big Christmas gala, Scrooge was too much a creature of discipline not to make at least an appearance. His presence wasn't required to inaugurate the festivities. Others would see to that. So he postponed ringing for Wilf as long as he could. He was angry that Belle was not there to accompany him. He would need to make some kind of excuse for her -- say she was sick, perhaps, or that she'd had a call from her daughter to come at once to the young woman's side. But

he couldn't be angry with her without also feeling guilty for his own behavior. If he hadn't been in such a pit of black despair, she wouldn't have felt the necessity of leaving him alone at Christmas to deal with his demons. Any way he looked at it, he was the one really to blame. The party, which had grown more gargantuan with every year, was in full swing when he arrived, with the noises of band music, dancing, and animated conversations spilling out into the vestibule of the hall. Almost the first person he encountered, after handing his coat and hat to the cloakroom attendant, was Mrs. Cratchit, who, despite the recentness of her husband's passing, was decked out in her usual festive Yuletide attire, a bright red blouse, a huge green skirt with multiple folds, and a great wooly Christmas tree of a vest, adorned with clever little handmade ornaments and with knitted packages at its base. Scrooge was somewhat shocked at the vision, given the brevity of her mourning period thus far, but said nothing as he accepted the cup of punch she handed him. "I'm glad you were able to come out, Mrs. Cratchit," he mumbled insincerely.

"Oh, I couldn't miss it," she exclaimed. "Bob, dear soul, would never forgive me iffen I did. It's what 'e woulda wanted, as sure as I'm standin' 'ere, Mr. Scrooge." She looked around, scouring the crowd. "But where's the missus? I'n't she comin' tonight?"

Scrooge attempted a faint smile as he said, "She couldn't make it, I'm afraid. Margaret needed her, and she's gone to be with her and Peter."

"Aw, poor thing," mourned Mrs. Cratchit. "I knows it's 'ard. I lost one meself oncet. Y' never git over it, long's ye live. Well, then, ye must come 'n' join Tim 'n' me at our table. Can't 'ave ye bein' alone on Christmas eve, can we? Not at y'r own party!"

Scrooge allowed himself to be led through the crowd to a table where Tim and some other young employees were sitting. Frankly, there wasn't much point in resistance. Mrs. Cratchit was a formidable woman, despite the brevity of her stature and the limitations of her grammar, if such the latter could be called.

He tried to make small talk with the young people, but knew he was failing miserably. Tim sensed it, and tried to atone by helping to carry the conversation along. At last, Mrs. Cratchit interrupted the pointless remarks with a declaration:"Ht's time you 'n' me 'ad a dance, Mr. Scrooge. In all these years, we've never taken a turn together. Now, with Bob gone and y'r missus away, it's time we did it. These younguns'll excuse us, won't ye? People will want to see th' head of

their fine company a-dancin', that's for sure. So come on, Mr. Scrooge. Let's show 'em a thing or two!"

It was clear that Mrs. Cratchit was not to be denied, so Scrooge yielded to the pressure she exerted on his arm as she tugged him toward the dance floor, where a reel was just ending and several couples were leaving for the refreshment bar. Soon the music commenced again, and the two of them were instantly engaged in the organized capers they had learned to execute in their earlier years, moving singly in and out, then joining hands and doing a quick side-step in unison with the others.

For a moment, Scrooge's spirit seemed to lift a little, for the dancing made him feel at least slightly better than he did before. It was only slightly, of course, and he was soon wondering what Belle would

think if she could see him and Mrs. Cratchit dancing now. She would laugh, he knew, and tease him about what a nimble dancer he was when paired with the redoubtable Missus C.

As the reel ended, the two of them moved aside and found a small table where they could sit alone. Scrooge excused himself and returned with two glasses of ale. "Whew!" breathed Mrs. Cratchit, "that was more activity that I've got up to since poor Bob fell sick. I wonder I didn't strain somethin' I shouldn't."

Scrooge half-smiled as he regarded her. "How do you do it?" he asked.

"Do what?"

"How do you carry on so bravely when you've lost your husband? I know you and Bob were as close as two people could ever be. You meant everything to one another. Oh, you both loved your children, I know that. But your love for one another came first. How many years had you been together?"

"You mean -- ?"

"Since you married. It's been about thirty years, hasn't it?"

Her eyes sparkled as she answered: "It would've been thirty-two iffen 'e 'ad lived only two more month."

Scrooge shook his head. "How do you bear it so well? You always fit together so well. How can you be so cheerful now, so soon after -- after he has gone? I mean, coming here tonight, wearing that -- that -- spectacular outfit. Smiling and laughing and dancing. Having a good time. So soon. I wasn't married to the man as you were, yet his passing has utterly devastated me. It wasn't just his, of course. I lost my friend Charles Dickens a few months ago too. And then you and I both lost a little grandchild. It's as if we're on a battlefield, and loved ones are dying all around us all the time. I only want to know how you can bear it the way you do."

She reached across and took one of his hands in both of hers. A look of enormous sympathy blossomed in her face.

"Oh, Mr. Scrooge," she said, sweetly and cooingly, as if speaking to a small child, "I know y'r 'urt. It hain't never easy t' let go o' someone ye love. I 'spect part o' y'r feelings is due t' the fack that ye ain't got no chilluns o' y'r own. That 'elps, y' know. I don't know wot I'd do w'out me Tim an' Peter an' Martha an' t'others. They 'elps t' remind me that it hain't all about me, y' know. Their young lives is a-goin' on almost as they would've if Bob was still 'ere. In your case, it's diff'rent. You and the missus ain't got no one else comin' along t' replace you when th' time comes. Well, the missus 'as, I know, but you ain't, Mr. Scrooge. An' it makes a diff'rence. I 'spect it makes a big diff'rence."

Chapter 21

Loss and Grief

Scrooge regarded her tenderly. She was a wise woman, and he appreciated what she had said. Perhaps having children did make a difference. He would never know, of course. On that subject, he could only speculate.

"Thank you, Mrs. Cratchit," he said with feeling. "You're a wonderful lady, and a very wise one. You're undoubtedly right. Children do make a difference. I'm sure of it. But I admire your spirit, madam. I

truly do. Bob never did a better day's work than the one when he won your hand in marriage. I've never known a man in all my years who was ever more anxious to get home at night than your Bob was each and every day. He could work for twelve hours, sometimes without even stopping for lunch or tea, and be so tired I thought he'd drop. But his step when he left the shop was always light and smart, as if the weariness all flew out of him the minute he started home. That was a remarkable tribute, I'd say -- a tribute to a fine woman and the comfort she gave her man."

Mrs. Cratchit blushed and ducked her head a little as she removed a handkerchief from her sleeve and dabbed at the small tears coursing down her cheeks. "Oh, Mr. Scrooge," she offered half in protest. "Thankee for sayin' that. I tried to be as good a wife as I knowed 'ow. I really did. An' what ye said -- y' know, 'bout Bob allays startin' home w' a light step -- well, I think that's th' way hit were w' 'im an' me. We was that close. An' y'r sayin' it brought it all back fer a minute. I felt as if 'e were 'ere, jus' like allays. Thankee, sir. Thankee fr'm th' bottom o' me 'eart!"

When they had finished their ale, Scrooge escorted Mrs. Cratchit back to Tim and his young friends, and excused himself to circulate and speak to a few other people before making his exit. He did shake some hands and wish a few associates Merry Christmas, but if anyone had been observing, it would have been plain that he was working his way toward the exit, where he soon reclaimed his hat and coat and walked out into the wintry evening. On his way, he pressed a guinea into the hand of one of the young factory workers he knew to be well acquainted with Wilf Tarkington, as he had once helped to load the lorries Wilf drove, and asked him to locate Wilf and tell him to stay as long as he liked, that Mr. Scrooge would make his own way home.

Normally, on Christmas eve after leaving the company party, Scrooge would have had Wilf drive him to the cemetery so he could say a few words to his old friend Marley, but somehow he wasn't in the mood tonight. He crossed the ends of his scarf across his chest and pulled the collars of his coat tightly together against the cold, deciding to walk the three or four miles to Russell Square. He knew he could hail a cab, but he needed to think, and he could think better on foot than in a taxi. His way led him past Piccadilly Circus and up Shaftesbury Avenue, where the city's theaters lay dark and empty for the holidays. His eye caught on an occasional marquee the name of an actor or actress he recognized. He passed a concert hall where he and Belle had enjoyed many performances by the London Symphony Orchestra, and noticed a brightly lit bookstore with customers streaming in and out, doubtless seeking last-minute Christmas presents for friends or family members. Pausing briefly before the store's window, he noticed displays of books by Thomas Macaulay, George Eliot, Elizabeth Barrett Browning, and, of course, Charles Dickens, all of whom were well known to him.

It was Belle, he reflected as he walked on, who had introduced him to these figures. His whole life, in recent years, revolved around her wit, her knowledge of cultural affairs, her acquaintance with people. It was she who had given him an interest in music and theater, she who had taught him the glory of the printed page. He was a man of finances and power, but it was she who had enlarged his awareness to include the humanities, who had led him to museums and concerts and readings, so that they were now an important part of his life. He was nothing without her, he thought, even less than nothing, for he was tormented without her. Why had he paid so little attention to her in recent months? How had he permitted the deaths of others to diminish the care and tenderness he accorded her? It was no wonder she had left him for Christmas. She needed a better atmosphere than the sepulchral pall his gloom had cast over their home. He should not even be surprised that she spent an increasing amount of time in the company of that glorified dandy, Captain Twiddle, for Tommy Q. Twiddle was buoyant and witty, and wore on his sleeve a sense of mild excitement about everything around him. He had noticed that Twiddle made her laugh, which was far more than could be said of him these past few months, who breathed only an air of graveyards and depression.

Mrs. Cratchit had the right attitude. Life is life, and goes on in spite of the little tragedies surrounding individual personalities. As he walked, observing the many people getting in and out of carriages, knocking on festively decorated doors, and, in some cases, huddling in little groups under street lamps to sing carols, he began to feel better and to find his inner balance again. Not perfectly, but enough to put a little more spring in his step as he turned onto Russell Square and beheld a number of carriages discharging their passengers into the Great Russell Hotel, where they doubtless intended eating and drinking and celebrating the holiday together, the way holidays should be celebrated.

Realizing he had eaten nothing since breakfast, not even at the party, he decided on impulse to dine at the hotel before returning to his empty house. The maître d' and most of the waiters at the hotel knew him, and they all showed their cheeriest faces and wished him Merry Christmas as he entered the dining room. He wasn't too pleased with the table they were able to give him at such short notice on a busy night, but he held his tongue, for he did not wish to alienate people who knew him. He ordered the duck, potatoes au gratin, green beans, and a cranberry salad, and washed it all down with a glass of bitter. Then he had coffee and a gooseberry tart as he sat and studied the other diners.

There were whole families who had obviously come for the sheer joy of dining in such an elegant environment on Christmas eve, and there was one large table surrounded by what appeared to be the members of some sales team or business group, including both wives and husbands. The latter were drinking heavily, chatting loudly, and frequently guffawing at things being said. Scrooge instructed his own waiter, a middle-aged man named Alfred who had often served him and Mrs. Scrooge, to go over and caution them that there were other guests present who would appreciate their observing a more proper decorum in a public dining room. The waiter seemed embarrassed to do it, but Scrooge held him to it, glaring at him throughout the procedure, and resolved not to leave him any tip at all unless he accomplished his mission.

One of the remarkable things about people who are at all miserable is that they cannot bear to be in the company of people who are not miserable, and, in spite of the slightly elevated mood in which he had arrived, Scrooge now felt sufficiently wretched again to want to get out of the restaurant. He could not take his mind off of Annabelle. All along, he had secretly hoped that she would relent and come home on Christmas eve, for surely she understood that she needed him, and, not to put too fine a point on it, deserved her more than Peter and Margaret, albeit Margaret was her daughter. People lost babies all the time, both in London and elsewhere. It was a fact of life that having a baby was a dicey business, and that there was always a fair chance of losing one at some point in the birth process. Why, he knew from his meetings of the various hospital boards he sat upon that the rate of such losses was appallingly high, especially among the working and lower classes. He couldn't remember the exact figures, but he knew they were astounding, particularly in the tenement houses and council flats of the East End. So why were

Peter and Margaret making such a fuss about their loss? Surely a couple of days would have been long enough for Annabelle to see that they were only using the premature birth of their baby as an excuse for self-pity and unnecessary pampering! Perhaps she was remaining where she was, he concluded, to upset him, to rub salt in his poor, wounded soul and cause him to be even more depressed than he had been. Well, confound it, it wasn't going to work! She could just stay where she was until Doomsday if she wanted to. Be it on her head for the course she had chosen! At last, tired of his mounting discomfort in the midst of all the joy and frivolity around him, Scrooge called for his bill, laid a couple of pounds on the plate to cover it, plus a minimal tip for the waiter, and demanded his hat and coat. It was a clear, starlit night, and he paused in the middle of Russell Square to look around at the hundreds of windows facing onto it. Many were lit with trees and candles, and he could see laughing, cheerful people entering and leaving the doorways of the big houses and apartment buildings. The general hubbub of the world around him only accentuated his own sense of loneliness and isolation, the fact that he was completely alone, without friends and family on that evening of evenings. The bile that had arisen in his spirit was corroding everything about him, especially his good sense and his earlier progress toward reasonableness and good will. He walked on through the square and tramped up the steps to his front door.

Funny, he thought. For an instant, his eye fell upon the huge door knocker brought from his former residence, and he could swear there was something strange about it, that, as it had on another Christmas eve so long ago, it bore for a fleeting moment the hazy image of his old friend and partner, Jacob Marley. He felt momentarily guilty that he had not bothered to visit Marley's tomb tonight. Surely that was all this quirky impression portended. He shook his head as if to clear his

vision. His mind must be going, he thought. The burdens of the past few months had put too great a strain upon it.

Unsettled, he inserted his key into the lock, turned it, and let himself in. The house was cold. He lit a fire in the library and another in his bedroom, grateful that Jason had prepared them with kindling and coal. He felt strange, as if something was happening inside him, something he could neither control nor understand. "Probably that duck," he thought to himself. "It tasted a little off." Having lit the fire in his bedroom, he changed into his night clothes, poked his feet into a pair of soft slippers Annabelle had given him two Christmases ago, and returned to the library, thinking he might read a book before retiring. He poured himself a brandy from the bottle on his desk, and looked about for something he might wish to read. Not finding anything that caught his interest, he carried his glass of brandy to an easy chair near the fire and sat to savor it as he stared into the flames.

He had not realized how tired he was. It had been a very long day, and then there had been the exertion of that reel with Mrs. Cratchit, as well as the long walk home. Halfway through the glass of brandy, he felt himself starting to nod off. as old men do. Once or twice, he caught himself and started awake. He set the brandy glass aside, fearful that he might forget and allow it to fall. The fire had finally warmed the room, and crackled softly and mesmerically in the grate. Overcome by weariness, he could feel himself slipping off.

Then, whether in a dream or in reality he would never know, he became somehow conscious of another presence, of someone speaking to him. Forcing himself to pay more attention, he became vaguely aware that there was someone or something in the easy chair on the other side of the room.

"Scroo-ooge."

He thought he heard the voice, and it startled him.

"Scroo-oo-ooge." it said again.

He focused more intently, hardly daring to do so, for fear of what he might behold. Still unable to see anything clearly, he reached for his brandy and took another sip. He would finish his drink and go to bed. The sooner he was asleep, the better!

"Scroo-oo-oooge!" This time, when he looked in the direction of the voice, his vision cleared and he saw him. Jacob Marley. Sitting there, as big as life -- though hardly as substantial -- in the chair that was twin to the one he himself did occupy.

"Marley!"

He could not believe his eyes.

"But -- but you're not! You can't be!"

Yet something in his head said that it was, he was, Marley, that is, for something like this had occurred before. Only this time, Marley was not encumbered by the vast and heavy chain he had worn on that earlier occasion. He sat there in his smoking jacket, calm as anything, puffing on a cigar that was far from insubstantial. In fact, it was one of Scrooge's own cigars, from a humidor on the desk not far from where he sat.

Chapter 22

Darkness Descends

"Jacob? What are you doing here? What's happening to me? What should I make of this?"

Calmly, Marley took another puff on his big cigar and blew some smoke rings before he deigned to make response. "You didn't come today. I expected you at the cemetery."

Then he shook his head slowly from side to side, the way one shames another who has done some great and grievous wrong.

"Why, Ebenezer?" he said.

"Why what, Jacob?" asked Scrooge.

"Why didn't you come? What is going on, old friend? You were doing so well. In fact, your behavior had become a great boon to me, probably without your knowing it. As you see, I no longer carry around those blasted chains." He waved his hand, the one holding the cigar, circularly in the air to display the degree of his freedom. "You see, you were atoning for me, old friend. Your good actions availed for both of us, and year by year my burden was lessened, until, quite recently, it was entirely canceled out."

C "I -- I --," stammered Scrooge. "I don't understand, Jacob."

Marley puffed again on the great cigar and blew more smoke rings. "No, you wouldn't," he said slowly and resignedly. "There are many things you don't understand, Scrooge. And you were doing so well, too."

"Jacob," said Scrooge, and hesitated. "You don't mean -- I mean --"

"The ghosts?" said Marley.

Scrooge nodded, apprehensively.

"I don't know about that, old man," said his former partner. Again Marley regarded the end of his cigar, which glowed eerily in the gathering gloom as the fire died away. He seemed to find some fascination in it.

"Say, these are good cigars," he said.

"Take them," said Scrooge. "Take all of them! They're yours, Jacob. Take anything you want -- whatever I have. It's all yours. Only please don't let them come again." Scrooge clasped his breast. "My heart won't take it. I'm older now, Jacob. I can't stand exertions, you know."

"I know, old man, but I don't have much say in these things." With those words, Marley rose, regarded the stub of a cigar he had smoked, and tossed it into the fireplace. Then he walked casually over to the humidor on the desk, removed another cigar, sniffed it, and walked off with it, right through the closed door.

Scrooge was flabbergasted. He put some more coal on the fire and sat to watch it catch and blaze against the bricks of the fireplace. He poured himself another glass of brandy and sat a while longer. Had he fallen asleep and dreamed that Marley was there? Or had it not been a dream at all? At last, as he heard a neighborhood clock strike twelve, he set down the empty glass he was holding, walked into his bedroom, climbed onto the bed, and fell fast asleep.

From time to time, he awoke to remember some dream or fragment of a dream he had just had and wonder if it was indeed a dream and not something more portentous. One was about Annabelle. She was coming down the aisle at their wedding on the arm of her father, old Fezziwig, only, when they drew near the altar, it wasn't old Fezziwig at all, but Captain Twiddle. Then, as Scrooge and Annabelle were moving up the aisle, arm in arm, at the end of the wedding, she suddenly and inexplicably metamorphosed into Mrs. Cratchit, who was wearing her red and green outfit from the office party. Baffled, Scrooge wondered what the dream could possibly mean. In another dream, he beheld himself as the demon of the counting house he had been before his transformation, and regretted his harsh, uncalled-for words to Bob Cratchit, who appeared to cower before him as a dog cowers before its master with a stick. Then he was accompanying the ghost of Christmas Yet-to-Come to a graveyard, where he beheld his own tombstone and recoiled as he had in the presence of that dreadful spirit so many years ago. Only, as he was leaving the scene, he noticed a woman sitting on a bench very near his grave, and a young man sitting beside her. The woman, veiled in black, he realized, was Belle, and she was weeping softly into her lace-edged handkerchief. The one beside her, who spoke now to comfort her, was young Tim Cratchit, his valet. "Don't cry, Missus Scrooge," he was saying as he laid a hand upon her arm. "It's been months now, and he wouldn't want you to suffer any more."

Sometime later, there was a crazy, mixed-up dream in which he was being knighted by Queen Victoria, and John Brown, the Queen's faithful consort for many years after the death of Prince Albert, was saying, "Let's go down to the pub for a pint, Scrooge. I want to consult with you about some investments." When they arrived at the pub, a party was in full swing. Making his way through the crowd with Brown, Scrooge suddenly realized he knew most of the people there. Many were employees at Marley, Scrooge, McDougall, & Cratchit, and they were toasting him as they sang, "For he's a jolly good fellow." Then he looked around for Brown and couldn't find him. But he did see Tommy Twiddle, and asked him if he'd seen Brown. "He's a good friend of mine," said Twiddle. "Is there anything I can do for you?" Then Annabelle was there, and asked him if he wasn't going to invite her to dance. He said no, he had something to show her, and, taking her out into the night air, he pointed to their big house on Russell Square, which was just across the road, and said, "It's yours, my dear. Would you like to see it now?" She said no, she couldn't, as her daughter needed her and she must go to her at once.

Although the details were hard to recall afterward, one dream involved Scrooge's good friend Dickens. They were on a back street somewhere in London, and the street lamps were burning very low, so that it was dark and shadowy. A woman approached them from a nearby doorway, her hand extended as if asking for money. As Scrooge got out his purse, Dickens suddenly slapped the woman on the cheek and told her to be gone. Puzzled, Scrooge asked if he knew the woman. "I have met her," he replied, "and we have had several children together. But I no longer wish to see her." Scrooge became angry with him over this brutish behavior and said he was going to his club. When he got there, he ran into the Prince of Wales, who told him that he had been right to leave Dickens because the woman Dickens had slapped was one of his mistresses.

Scrooge knew there had been another dream or two, and he tried to recall them when he awoke to go to the bathroom, but he could not. While he was up, he heard the sonorous tolling of the neighborhood bell and counted the tolls. One... two... three... For a moment he was startled, as his mind reverted to that earlier occasion when one of the Christmas spirits, the silent and most frightening one, came calling on him. Could it be? Was it happening again? he wondered. But they were merely dreams. Or were they? Troubled, he trundled back to his bed, crawled in, and hauled up the covers.

This time he could not get back to sleep. Too many thoughts tumbled over one another in his head. Annabelle... Bob Cratchit... Dickens... Mrs. Cratchit at the Christmas party . . . young Tim . . . the Tarkingtons out in their carriage house . . . the crowds of people he had beheld on yesterday's streets.

Christmas . . . . It was already Christmas day! He remembered that fateful night before Christmas when he had been visited by

Marley's ghost and the three spirits. Marley! He thought about the vision he had had of his former partner only last night, in this very house, in his library, smoking a cigar and complaining about Scrooge's behavior in recent months. It was all a jumble. Life itself was a jumble. How to sort it out? How did people ever manage to make sense of their lives? Time dragged on, and still he could not tame the unruliness of his thoughts, which continued to pop up erratically like dozens of hares and then dart wildly over the landscape. He had had such crazy times before, but none so extreme as this. Was this what it was like to die? Did one's mind simply go

haywire at the end, discharging volleys in every direction and striking nothing? He wished he could get it over with. The waiting was excruciating.

At last, though, his mind stopped churning so madly on a spate of topics. Instead, it seemed to focus upon a single thought, that perhaps his life was much better than he had lately estimated. He was still married to darling Annabelle, albeit she was at her daughter's now. His business interests were prospering, his companies continuing to expand. He was highly regarded by the public for his many charitable endeavors. He had an unblemished record of church attendance for several years, and stood in happy relationship to the vicar, Mr. Plumwood, and to Mrs. Plumwood as well. He and Belle lived in a beautiful home, where they were served by a staff of good and faithful attendants. He had lost his dear friends Bob Cratchit and Charles Dickens, to be sure, but both were well composed at the end and their actual suffering had been minimal as such things go. He himself, and Belle as well, were in sound physical condition, or believed themselves to be. There was nothing really wanting to their happiness. Nothing except that they should be happy, and enjoy the estate to which his labors and commitments had brought them. He had been insufferable these past few months, it was true, grieving for those he could not hold, impatient with his role as mortal bystander, a whiner and complainer who had no intrinsic right to such happiness as was naturally his, if he only acknowledged and embraced it.

In the end, he prayed that God would forgive him for being such a ninny and give him a chance to straighten out his attitudes, much as a shopkeeper orders his wares at the end of day in preparation for the store's reopening the next morning. He would go to Belle as soon as it was daylight and beg her forgiveness for his behavior. They would be happy again, and their home would once more shine with the illustrious dinners and parties that had so distinguished it in the past. As soon as possible, they would invite the Queen herself to dine with them, and he would present special gifts to all her retinue, even the footmen and carriage drivers. It was time he and Belle were out in society again, going to the opera she loved so dearly and attending the theater at least weekly or bi-weekly. With every resolution his heart felt lighter, as if it might simply float away on all these pleasant ruminations. And soon he had fallen to sleep once more, this time without any puzzling or enervating dreams, at least none of which he was aware, for it was a deep and peaceful slumber, untroubled, so far as he could remember afterwards, by a single thought.

Until --

There was Belle again. He could just make out her face. She was in one of her floral hats, the purple one, he thought, and there was a beautiful, soft fur thrown about her shoulders. She was lovely, he thought. Now she was reaching out to him, speaking to him, calling his name.

"Ebbie . . . Ebbie, wake up!" she was saying. "I'm home."

Chapter 23

Christmas Eve Alone

It took a moment or two for him to realize he wasn't dreaming, that it was now daylight, the curtains had been drawn back, and the woman before him was real and not a specter. "Ebbie," she said as she gently stroked his cheek, "wake up, dear! It's me. I'm home. It's Christmas, sweetheart. It's our anniversary. The most special day of the year. Do you remember? We were married on Christmas. I couldn't miss this day with you."

"Wha -- ?" Scrooge shook his head, attempting to clear it. "Belle? You're home? But -- but -- how? Did you just get here? How did you come? Did Wilf -- ?" "No, silly. I didn't want to disturb Wilf. I sent word to Tommy last night, and he gallantly rose early and brought us back this morning." "Us?"

"Yes, dear. Peter and Margaret came as well. And Tommy's down in the drawing room with them."

Scrooge was now sitting up, his hands propped behind him, and his gaze was growing steadier. It was obvious that he was still trying to make sense of everything.

"Come on," said his wife, "get up, you lazybones! Can't you smell what's cooking? As we arrived, Mrs. Cratchit and Tim and Martha were just stepping out of a taxi. She didn't know I would be here, and thought you should have a proper Christmas breakfast, so she came along with Tim and Martha to prepare it. And no sooner had she got into the kitchen than the back door opened and there were Mrs. Tarkington and Jennifer, with the same objective. So they're all in there now, bustling about and preparing a lot of food. You'd better get up and dress, or you'll hold up everything. Oh, Wilf and Jason will be joining us as well. They've been tending to the horses."

Temporarily discombobulated by this flow of information, Scrooge nevertheless put his feet out from under the covers and onto the floor, and it wasn't long before he had washed and shaved and dressed. When he went downstairs, he found the rooms below resounding with lively, eager conversations, and saw Jennifer, Martha, and Tim bustling about with plates of food on their way to the dining room. "There's the man!" came a vibrant voice. It belonged to Captain Twiddle, who was just leaving the drawing room with Peter and Margaret Cratchit on their way to the dining room. "Glad to see you up and about, old fellow! Having a good snooze, were you?"

"Oh, hello, Twiddle," said Scrooge, extending his hand. The captain shook it enthusiastically, while clapping him on the arm with his other hand. "Merry Christmas, " he said with feeling. "It's a great day, Ebenezer, and I'm happy to be included in this fashion!"

When the entire crowd were assembled around the long dining table, with Belle at one end and Scrooge at the other, Scrooge suggested that they all hold hands and ask Tim to say a blessing. Tim gladly did so, concluding his prayer with the words, "God bless us every one!"

Mrs. Tarkington said she would continue presiding over the sideboard, which was laden with ham, eggs, sausages, potatoes, beans, fried mushrooms, tomatoes, fried bread, plain bread, butter, and several kinds of jam, and insisted that Mrs. Cratchit, who had served so energetically in the kitchen, should take a seat with the others, which she did, next to Belle and her daughter Martha. Soon they were all eating and chattering as if they hadn't seen one another in ages, and Scrooge was still trying to come to terms with his surprise that the day had begun as it had.

"Oh!" said Mrs. Cratchit, pushing back her chair and rushing into the kitchen. "I almost forgot the blackberry wine," she burbled as she returned bearing two large flagons. "Martha, Jennifer, would you

please bring some more glasses? I made it meself, an' was a-savin' it fer jus' such an occasion as this. I almost forgot it, what wi' my husband's passin' an' all, but I remembered jus' as we was a-gittin' in th' carriage, an' sent Tim back t' fetch it. It should taste jus' right wi' this wonderful ham an' sausage."

"Nectar of the gods," proclaimed Scrooge when he had taken a sip. "You've outdone yourself again, Mrs. Cratchit."

"To Mrs. Cratchit," said Captain Twiddle, cheerily hoisting his wine glass in her direction. "A vintner of the first rank!"

"Hear, hear!" added Scrooge as they all lifted their glasses in a salute to the obviously pleased and grinning Mrs. Cratchit.

A gracious bonhommie had settled on the entire room, and each person seemed to enjoy the company of all the others. More than once, Scrooge felt like pinching himself to see if it was truly a reality, or merely some clever illusion his mind was practicing upon him. Only yesterday he had been so miserable, yet now his heart was near to bursting, having Belle home and being surrounded at this joyous table by such happy friends and associates. He noticed that even Peter and Margaret had become surprisingly light-hearted and were bantering with the other young people as if no longer subdued by their recent sad experience. And young Tim—Tim was shining as if the sun itself had taken up residence behind his face! Consulting his pocket watch, the one bearing the same golden fob he had once "lost" in an alley, Scrooge announced. "Ah, it's almost ten o'clock. If we can throw a cloth over the food, ladies, and leave the cleaning up till later, we can just make it to St. Martin's for worship at eleven. Some can travel in the carriage with Wilf and Missus Scrooge and me, and others in Captain Twiddle's conveyance, if that's all right with you, Tommy."

At the church, there was a lively singing of hymns and carols by a spirited congregation, and the Rev. Mr. Plumwood was unaccustomedly merciful in the brevity of his sermon, owing, as was clearly evident, to a sore throat and some difficulty in speaking. Afterwards, following a general round of greetings, the party that had come from the Scrooges' packed themselves into the two carriages once more, and, at Scrooge's direction, journeyed to the distribution point of one of his many food charities, this one upon Oxford Street, where they joined in serving the poor who streamed through the noisy facility for the next three hours. The meal was of a basic, traditional nature, with baked turkey, dressing and gravy, mashed potatoes, yams, broad beans, baked beans, cranberry sauce, great loaves of bread served with butter and jellies, and, for dessert, a choice of pumpkin, apple, or mincemeat pie, all provided with ample supplies of tea and coffee. Scrooge stood beside Mrs. Cratchit for the slicing and serving of the turkeys, and seeing her at this task reminded him of the Christmas many seasons ago when he appeared at the Cratchit household bearing an oversized turkey to replace the meager bird that Bob had purchased the night before. "Hey, guv'nor," said one rough-looking man on whose plate Scrooge had just plopped a succulent piece of white meat, "wot's wi' this pale stuff?! Gimme one of them legs there, if y' don't mind." Before Scrooge could open his mouth to speak, Mrs. Cratchit answered for him: "Be on yer way, buster, an' be grateful fer wot ye received. Waddya think this is, Christmas?"

"Oh, Missus Cratchit," intervened Scrooge, "it is Christmas, and he's right, you know. I wasn't paying attention. He looks like a true dark-meat customer if I ever saw one. Very sorry, sir. Let me add this juicy leg to the slab of delicious white meat you already have, and a Merry Christmas to you."

Silently staring at Mrs. Cratchit, the man nodded his head in Scrooge's direction and moved along, where Peter Cratchit doused the meat, both white and dark, with a liberal serving of gravy, to which his wife Margaret added a very large helping of dressing.

"Blimey," said another man passing through the line a bit later, "ain't you that Scrooge fellow, the one in Mr. Dickens's book? I seen y'r picture in the paper a coupla times, an' thought I recognized ye. Y'er Sir Endicott or somethin' now, ain't ye? Congratulations and best wishes, I'm sure!"

Scrooge's heart, as always, was touched with pity as he looked into the faces of the needy persons passing before him -- old women with frightened eyes and scraggly hair springing out from under hard-used woolen hats, old men who appeared tired and listless and on their last legs, little children wide-eyed with wonder at the sight of so much food, mothers looking grateful to know that their little ones were receiving a healthy meal for a change, even the occasional toff in fine clothes, which, by the look of them, had been slept in in some filthy alleyway because their owner was down on his luck. "Bless you, " Scrooge would say to some, and "Merry Christmas!" he called to others. Whatever reservations about Christmas he might have held in recent days, he was now immersed in the kind of broken and needy humanity that would redirect the soul of even a hardened reprobate to thoughts of God and gratitude.

From time to time, when the flow of indigents slowed to a crawl, those serving the dinners found a minute or two to help themselves to a bit of food, and all of them swore that it tasted better, under the circumstances, than a five-course meal at a pricey city restaurant. "Those apple tarts is plumb delicious!"

young Tim Cratchit was heard to say, to which his mother made reply, "They hain't 'alf bad, son, iffen I do say so meself. I wouldn't mind askin' one o' th' cooks fer th' receipt."

When the serving was over and they all departed for their homes, Captain Twiddle said he would drop off the Cratchits, including Peter and Margaret, at Mrs. Cratchit's house before going to call on friends he had promised to visit on Christmas day. When Scrooge and Belle and the Tarkingtons climbed into the handsome carriage Wilf was driving, Scrooge asked if the others would mind a slight diversion on their way back, and, when they assured him they wouldn't, requested that Wilf drive through the cemetery so he could make a brief stop at Marley's grave. When they neared the spot from which old Marley's statue was visible, he directed Wilf to wait and told the others he would be but a short time paying his respects to his former partner.

"Here I am, Jacob," he said as he took his place on the stone bench opposite the statue. "I apologize for last night, old man, when I wasn't at my best. I'd had too much to drink, I'm sure, and was all but asleep when you popped in. I'm still not certain you were there, you know, but I believed you were, and would in fact have sworn it. You smoked one of my cigars, remember? And you said you were disappointed in me lately, for I was beginning to put you in danger of getting back your chains. Well, whether you were there or not, my friend, you were right. I have been guilty of a very poor spirit of late. I'm sorry for that, and promise to do better in the future. I had some things wrong in my head, you know -- all the death and disappointment around me sort of put me off my game. Seeing you, as always, helped to set me straight again. I think I'm all right now. Thanks, dear partner. I don't know what I'd do without you."

Epilogue: "The Divine Connectivity"

That evening, after Scrooge and Belle had consumed some bread and tea and were quietly nursing their brandies before a blazing fire, he offered a second apology, this one to Belle for the way he had been behaving of late. He had already proffered it several times since her arrival in the morning, but this time it was more protracted and explanatory. He spoke at length of how devastated he had been by the deaths of Bob Cratchit and Dickens, and then, of course, Peter and Margaret's little unborn child.

"I had looked forward to being a grandfather, at least sort of," he said. "It seemed so fitting, in the midst of the other dying, for something to be born that was fresh and, well, compensatory. Then, for the child to die before it was given even the slightest opportunity of living—" He paused. "It seemed somehow macabre, a mocking of life and the natural order of things. All that mortality simply shook me to the very depths, for what it kept reminding me of, at bottom, was that we too are going to die, you and I. I don't matter so much, my dear. I've had a good, full life, far more than I had any right to expect. But it mattered to me that you might die. I couldn't bear the thoughts of that, and yet I could not stop thinking about it."

"Oh, Ebbie," she said, "I know! I know! I think of it too -- that one of us will die, and the other be left alone after all we've meant to one another. How devastatingly lonely I would be were it you who left me. I can't imagine what I'd do. My life has changed so much since you reentered it. This house, these dear, dear servants, the people we've entertained, St. Martin's Church, our function in society at large -- the significance of all of them would shift completely if you were no longer at my side. It would be devastating. But we can't think that way, my dear. We must, each of us, continue to live with the joy and excitement that have become our wont. Otherwise, we shall have given in to death before its time, and missed so much that is still ours to cherish."

Chapter 24

Redemption and Joy

Scrooge looked into the lovely face whose contours constantly altered in the flickering light from the fire.

"Oh, my darling, you are so right," he said. "I was living in such fear of everything's collapsing around me that I had given up already, and was inwardly dying for fear of what might transpire. But I'm all right now, my sweet. Do not fear that I shall fall into my old morbidity. It was like a sickness, but, now that the fever has crested and gone, I have become as I should have been all along."

He told her about his "visit" from Marley, and the panoply of dreams which reminded him of that earlier Christmas when he received the visits of a trio of spirits. "Taken all together," he said, "they enabled me to see what in my misery I had been missing, that all life is connected, like some never-ending drama on a stage where everyone plays his part as others are playing theirs. And, though we are diminished by the loss of players around us, and continually threatened by the possibility that our own roles may soon be terminated, the play, the glorious play, goes on. The greatest sin in life, I believe, is not to see that, and to be despondent because we assume, when our fellow actors make their exits, or when we ourselves must desert the boards, that the play itself is being taken down. It isn't! The play goes on! The action may shift from scene to scene, and there are periods of greater and lesser intensity in the plotting, but there is no end to the mighty drama itself. God sees to that."

They sat quietly, listening to the whisper of dying ashes falling upon others in the hearth.

"I remember when Arthur died," said Belle at last. "I thought my world had ended. An old clergyman who lived on the block nearby, a Mr. Bales, I think his name was, came to sit with me one

afternoon. We talked of little things as we had our tea. And then, when the tea was drunk and the biscuit plate was almost empty, the conversation turned very deep and mellow. 'Mrs. Moore,' he said, his voice quite solemn and full of pathos, 'we must always remember the Divine Connectivity.' 'Divine Connectivity,' I thought. I'd never heard of that. But he went on to speak of it at length -- how everything in God's universe is somehow linked to everything else, so that anything that happens, however slight, is felt, however mildly, in every other part. 'That is our comfort,' he assured me, 'that everything that is is interconnected, so that we are never alone, whatever befalls us and whosoever passing we are fated to mourn.' I have often thought of those words and repeated them to myself. They were a great comfort to me in the loss of my husband. And, to be honest, dear Ebbie, they were part of what persuaded me that I should marry you, for they helped me to feel, as you expressed it so well a moment ago, that you and I, and Celia and Margaret, and everyone else were mere parts of some ongoing, eternal drama that we can never interrupt, or have a right to do so."

For a minute or two, Scrooge said nothing. Annabelle thought perhaps he had fallen asleep. "Ebbie?" she said, inquiringly.

"Darling!" he suddenly exclaimed. "That's it! You have helped me to remember. There was another dream! I had forgotten. I knew I was missing something, something of great significance, and you have helped me to remember!"

As the fire burned lower, he eagerly related the forgotten dream.

"It was about myself all those years ago -- myself as a schoolboy, as shown to me by the spirit. And Fan, my dear sister! She was there too. Fan as a little girl. And young Tim Cratchit -- he was in it too, somehow. Not as he is now, but as he was when the spirits brought him so powerfully to my attention, as a poor, crippled child, before the doctor had ever treated him. And Margaret's little premature baby. And the Child laid in a manger. He was part of it too. In fact, he was the center of it, the reason for everything! It was all connected! That's why your phrase 'divine connectivity' brought it back to me just now!

"It is all connected, my dear! Jesus and Mary and the children . . . Margaret's baby . . . And Margaret is your baby! Don't you see?! That's what it's all about! It's why Dickens was so greatly interested in children, I think! They're the key! Maybe he didn't exactly see it, but they are. It's why Christmas is so important. We all revert to childhood at Christmas, and want to behave as youngsters. We may not realize it, but Christmas reminds us of our connections, our ties to something we never outgrow, no matter how long we live. That's the missing link! It's what we fail to see, why we don't realize the holiday is so important. Oh, of course it's a lot of fun. But it is much more than that. It's the key to everything about us -- the way we want the world to be. Oh, Belle, you've done it! You've shown me what it's all about. And to think I almost missed it again!"

"Oh Ebbie, dear," said Belle, impressed by his torrent of words. "It sounds so logical! That must be true!"

"The children are the key," Scrooge continued, thinking aloud. "It's why you simply had to go to Margaret in her need -- and why people sometimes behave foolishly and irresponsibly at Christmas." He was thinking of the troublesome people at the restaurant. "Of course! It's why we center on the manger scene and the homage of the wise men. It's all about children. It's why Father Christmas is important around the world. He enables us to become children again, to focus on what we need to see in order to be renewed."

Belle squeezed his hand. She could tell there was no stopping the spate of words pouring from Scrooge's mouth, for his mind was on fire.

"Foundling hospitals!" he said, as if they suddenly became the focus of his thoughts. "Little children with no homes. Belle, I must devote more energy to them. I know! Let's establish a chain of foundling homes throughout the country, so that there is one in every little town in England. Let's call them 'The Annabelle Scrooge Homes for Children.' They will become known all over the world, and remind everybody of the importance of children. Oh my dear, thank you! Thank you, thank you, thank you! You have helped me to retrieve the most important dream of all, the one at the center of everything."

Once more there was a pause, in which an agreeable silence prevailed, broken only by the occasional hiss of some lone ember falling through the grate.

"I am so fortunate," Scrooge said at last, "to have been given so many opportunities! To work for your father and fall in love with his daughter. Then, having muffed that opportunity, to find you again and be given a second chance. And finally, more recently, when I was failing so miserably and could have spoiled everything, especially the happiness of our home and marriage, to be offered one last opportunity to become the person I should never have ceased to be, and to set things right before it is too late. It isn't too late, my love. In fact, I feel as if we're about to enjoy a whole new beginning, a chance to live with even more joy and fervor than before.

"There are so many things yet to do -- so many people to help, so many interesting folks to meet, and so many delightful years to spend together. Let's begin tomorrow, love! Let's plan a big New Year's party, an enormous one, and invite a lot of people we hardly know. Let's schedule trips to places we have never been. Let's vow right now to let no day go by without celebrating it!" She smiled as the light continued to play upon her features, though dimly now, for the fire was almost gone. "Thank God," she said, "you're back, Ebbie. My dear Ebbie. You're truly back!"

"By the way," he added, "while we're planning that party, let's be sure to invite Tommy Twiddle."

"Tommy?" she asked, somewhat surprised.

"Yes. We had a delightful conversation today. I think Tommy would be the perfect person to head up a new charity I've been thinking about -- a society for old soldiers. You know, to assure that they have all the medical help and other things they need. Tommy was in the military. He understands these things. He sounded as if he'd be quite interested."

At last they fell into a time of more or less idle chatter, making up for the days they had been apart. Margaret and Peter were much improved, Belle thought, and already talked of trying to have another baby. Tim Cratchit had told Scrooge he would be back the following day to resume his employment as Scrooge's valet. He hoped that would be all right, and Scrooge told him it would be perfect. Gertrude Tarkington had agreed to fill in as cook for a few days, so Mrs. Holyrood would not have to cut her visit short. Belle would need to shop for a new dress for their gala New Year's party. Scrooge said he noticed in passing through the theater district the night before that their old friend William Gilbert was collaborating with some fellow named Sullivan or Sutherland -- he couldn't remember which -- on a new musical comedy, and Belle said they must try to go one night.

When their glasses were empty and the conversation had run its course, they sat once more without speaking. At last, Scrooge reached out and took Belle's hand, the one that bore the simple gold ring he had bought her so many years ago, and held it lightly. "I'm a very lucky man," he said, "and can't imagine a better life than the one I have."

They felt themselves enveloped in a mutual aura of love and satisfaction. At last, Belle spoke, assuming that she must be the one to initiate their getting up to go to bed. "That Tim," she said as she stood up, "is becoming a fine young man, isn't he, Ebenezer?"

"Mmm-mm," said Scrooge, only half awake.

"I really liked something he said in his blessing this morning."

"Mmm," murmured Scrooge again, commencing his struggle to rise from the easy chair.

"How did he put it? 'God bless us every one.' That was sweet, wasn't it, love?"

"Yes, yes. Very sweet," he said, stretching in an upright position. "I want to remember that. Perhaps I shall write it in my diary."

Scrooge said nothing, but there was a little smile on his face. He was very sure he would remember. He had heard it before.

About the Author

Reverend Killinger was a graduate of Baylor University and earned his Theological Degree at Harvard Divinity School. He also has a PhD from the University of Kentucky, and PhD from Princeton Theological Seminary.

He began his pastoral experience in rural Baptist church in Kentucky, eventually becoming senior minister of the First Presbyterian Church of Lynchburg, VA., the First Congregational

Church of Los Angeles, and the famous Marble Collegiate Church in New York City, where Norman Vincent Peale was the minister for more than forty years. He has taught at several major universities, including Vanderbilt, Chicago and Princeton, and has lectured all over the U.S. and abroad. A prolific writer, he is the author of over 90 books.

John's entire life was dedicated to serving God and his congregation. John was a humble man and opened his heart to everyone. He enjoyed counseling people and later in retirement was still sought after to give sermons and lectures. He had a passion for the theatre, loved nature and bird watching, a challenging crossword puzzle, playing cards, and the social aspect of frequently having lunch out with family and friends.